The Widow's Retreat

AJ Carter

Papyrus
PUBLISHING

Dedication

For my wife, who keeps my dreams alive.

For my daughter, who inspires me to dream bigger.

For my dog, who farts in her sleep.

The Widow's Retreat

by AJ Carter

Prologue

I F I KNEW this was how I would die, I never would have taken this trip.

It'd started as a free ticket, but now my son and I are stuck at the top of an abandoned watchtower. There's nobody around for miles, save for the people on the ground trying to kill us. We haven't heard a peep from them in a few minutes, but they're still there.

They must be.

Hayden is snuggled into me, the pale moonlight drawing attention to the tears on his cheeks. He finished crying a while ago, but they're still there, crystallising under his raw eyes. I wipe them away with my thumb, still pressing my foot hard onto the trapdoor that leads to the only ladder.

He's looking at me like I can save him, but I'm not sure I can.

'It's going to be okay,' I say to him.

But that's a lie. We're only slightly higher than the trees that surround us, and the nearest town is so far away I can't even see it from here. Sean went for help a long time ago, and he should be back by now. It's time I start accepting that we're going to die.

It quickly becomes a reality when I start to smell smoke. It's creeping up the ladder and seeping through the trapdoor. At first, I thought it was my mind playing a nasty trick on me, but when I start to cough, I realise with absolute certainty that our pursuers are going to get us – that they've started a fire to smoke us out, and the only way out is down.

One way or another, we're going to die.

Chapter 1
Now

CHRISTMAS IS the hardest time of year for us. There are bright, colourful lights that shine all the way up the London streets. Buses are plastered with Christmas ads, shop windows are filled with seasonal sales, and the TV is basically a no go due to the overwhelming number of festive films. We can't even go into supermarkets without a stack of mince pies blocking our paths, so how on earth are we supposed to avoid it?

It's simple – we can't.

I didn't make it any easier on myself by coming to Harrods, but my son is eight years old, and if anyone deserves a jaw-dropping gift, it's him. It's been five years since he lost his dad – murdered on Christmas Day – but the memory is still raw for both of us. In fact, I was underselling it when I said Christmas is a hard time for us.

The truth is, it's absolute torture.

Inside Harrods, I make my way to the correct floor and wait in line to collect my reserved item. Hayden begged for a PlayStation 5, and I've been telling him they're too hard to find. It's actually true, and I only managed to reserve this one because I have a friend on the inside, but I can't wait to see his face when he opens it. Hopefully, it'll be quite the shock.

After an hour or so of waiting in the extremely long queue, the man at the counter brings out a giant white box that I'm not sure how to carry home. I decide immediately that I'll need an Uber, as there's no way I'm lugging that thing around on the Tube.

The Uber comes in a white saloon. The driver actually exits the vehicle to help me with the Play-Station, which I'm very grateful for as it's starting to hurt my back. Throughout the journey, he makes idle chatter about his family and how this is his busy season. I nod politely, although he can't see me, then try to enjoy the journey with my eyes closed. I don't think I'm very tired – I just don't want to see any more of Christmassy London.

It's just another reminder of what we lost.

IT ONLY TAKES ten minutes to drive, but December traffic easily doubles it. When we arrive outside my flat on Marylebone, the driver's voice actually wakes me up when he announces that our transaction has ended. I try to hide the fact I was sleeping, but my eyes still need rubbing. I exit the car and meet him at the back, where he helps carry the box to my door.

'Thanks so much for your help,' I tell him.

'No problem,' he says, saluting lazily. 'Remember that when you tip.'

I laugh and roll my eyes, but I'll tip him anyway. It's a habit by now, unless the service is completely terrible. When the driver leaves, I let myself in and take the lift to the penthouse. Our flat is the only one on this floor, but there's still a corridor between the lift and the front door. I head down it with caution, praying Hayden doesn't see his gift unwrapped.

Letting myself in, I set the PlayStation by my feet and lean through the front door. Hayden's high-pitched voice carries as he squeals with delight, playing with Chloe, the babysitter. I call into the flat, asking her to come. She barely hears me over all the fun they're having, but when she does, they both come running. I pull the door closer, leaving very little room for my tiny body.

'Are you all right?' Chloe asks, frowning. She's twenty-two and beautiful, with perfect golden locks and stunning blue eyes, but the frown does her no justice. She suddenly looks ten years older but still pretty, I suppose.

'I'm fine,' I tell her. 'Can you put Hayden to bed?'

'It's still early,' Hayden complains from behind the door.

'It's eight o'clock, and you have school tomorrow.'

'But I don't want to.'

'Well, I don't want to have lower back pain, but life is unfair like that.'

Chloe laughs and takes him away, leading him to his room by making it a game of chase. I heave the box into my arms and hurry it into my bedroom, instantly noticing the warm smell of spaghetti sauce coming from the kitchen. Easy meals only, I'd told Chloe, and she seems to have followed my instruction as usual.

The penthouse is a three-bedroom elegant

home with white marble and plenty of space. It's all white with modern worktops and furniture that makes it look almost space-age. In the daytime, we get all the sunlight we need from the wide windows and skylights. In the night, we have a beautiful view of the London skyline. But we keep the curtains closed at Christmas. The last thing we need is yet another reminder. It's the same reason we don't do decorations.

When Nick died, we almost moved out. I look back on the decision and realise how close a call it was. There was no way I could afford the mortgage here, so we used to rent. One day, without warning, the landlord announced he was selling the flat. I put the inheritance from Nick and put it with my own savings, bought the place outright. My guardian angel must have been looking out for me, Sean keeps saying. He's my boyfriend, who lives with us now, but he isn't home from work yet.

I head back into the hall and thank Chloe, paying her the usual rate along with a bonus for Christmas. There are still three weeks to go, but I can't see myself needing her services until the new year, so there's a small tip in there for her. Just enough to buy herself a couple of drinks next time she celebrates. I appreciate her making a big deal of it.

'Thank you,' she says warmly, shouldering her handbag. 'If you need me, just call.'

'Will do. Have a great Christmas.'

'You, too. Oh. You had some letters. I put them on the coffee table.'

I nod and say goodbye, just now realising how long I was gone. The day started with meeting an old friend for lunch, but after taking a walk and going for a quiet drink to clear my head, I then called Chloe to see if I could come home later. She was happy to oblige because it was extra money, so that gave me a little freedom for the evening.

Before bed, I go to see Hayden in his room. It's decorated with all things Marvel and Fortnite, though I don't know why he did the latter as it's a video game he doesn't have access to. Not until he opens his present, anyway. The posters cover the entire wall above his bed, where he's sitting up and reading something with wolves on the cover.

'Good book?' I ask, perching on the end of his bed. I start stroking his silky hair, but it doesn't seem to knock his concentration. His beady little eyes are focused hard on the story. 'I picked up your Christmas present today.'

Suddenly, he looks up. 'What is it?'

'A surprise. You'll have to wait.'

'Then why tell me at all?'

It's hard not to laugh at how snarky he can be sometimes. An outsider would think he has an attitude, but it's really just a part of his fun personality. After his father died, I really worried he'd have a chip on his shoulder for the rest of his life, but if anything, it just toughened him up. Then again, I sometimes hear him crying in the night. Always at Christmas.

'Do you need anything?' I ask. 'Water?'

'No, thanks. Night, Mum.'

'Goodnight.'

Stepping out to the hallway, I close his door and sink into the living room sofa, exhaling slowly. It's hard being a mum, but even harder when your son is reaching the age where he's taking other interests. I distract myself by going through the mail, shuffling letters around to give myself a preview of what to expect. It's all the usual: bills, catalogues, a Christmas card from a friend who hasn't otherwise said a word to me in fifteen years.

And something else that catches my eye.

My brow furrows as I set the other things aside and touch the thick card with gold lining. Just more junk, I think at first, when I open it and see I've won a prize. How many of these do we get a year? Ten? I'm about to throw it out when I notice it actually has my name on it. No *Dear Customer* or *To the Lucky Winner*. It actually says:

Congratulations, Kate Bailey!

I read the card in full, seeing that we've won a trip to Scotland. There's a cottage in Deepwood, which is apparently the perfect place for isolation. The place looks nice and atmospheric, but the draw for me is that it's away from London. Better yet, it's during Christmas. I want to believe this is real, so I call the number with caution and get ready to hang up, but when the man answers to tell me I don't need to give any additional details, it quickly becomes clear this is the real thing. I can hardly believe my luck – not because I can't afford a trip or have never won anything before, but because this is the excuse I needed.

If we're lucky, we just might get to escape Christmas this year.

. . .

I'm PRACTICALLY BOUNDING at Sean as he walks in the door. He's dressed out of his police officer's uniform and is now wearing simple jeans and a T-shirt under a long, beige coat. He barely puts his bag down before I engulf him in a hug. I don't know what's come over me. It seems pitiful, really, but just the idea of not having to see another damn Christmas light feels like it might change everything. Even if it is just for one year.

'Slow down, cowgirl,' he says, laughing as he hugs me back.

'I can't. I'm too excited! Here, let me explain.'

Prising away from his athletic body, I take his hand and lead him into the living room. We sit with the small glasses of wine I prepared for us, and then I proceed to tell him all about the win. He listens with polite silence, studying me with those emerald eyes. Even now, after three years together, I'm still noticing how handsome he is. It's the chiselled jaw and the youthful features, even though he is hovering around his mid-thirties along with myself.

When I finish talking, he rubs his chin and lowers his gaze to the floor. I'm actually a little disappointed that he's not as into this as I am, but maybe I can talk him round.

Maybe.

'Are you sure it's legit?' he asks.

'Yep, I called and confirmed, then ran it through Google.'

'Is this really how you want to spend Christmas?'

'Away from all the awful reminders? Far, far away from all the glitter and crappy festive films?' I nudge him playfully. 'Yes, it's exactly how I want to spend it. It'll be good for Hayden, too. The poor kid has been through so much.'

Sean nods thoughtfully, then examines the card again. I know what he's thinking – that he might not be able to get time off work. The police station tends to steal him away from me as much as possible, especially at this time of year. But he works so hard that I wonder if they might be lenient on him just this once.

'You know this is miles from town, right? If you change your mind...'

'I won't. My heart is already set on this.'

'Have you had time to think it through, or is this reactionary?'

Shaking my head ever so slightly, I climb on top of him, cupping his face in my hands as I kiss him gently on the lips. 'We need this, Sean. We haven't been away at all since we met, and Hayden's fed up with being locked up in a flat whenever he's not at school. If there's only one thing I'll ever ask you for, this is it. Please.'

It feels like a lifetime before he meets my gaze. When he finally does, his frown lifts and transforms into a pleasant smile that somehow brings more light to his eyes. He opens his mouth as if to speak, hesitates, then tries again.

'Okay,' he says. 'Let's do it.'

Chapter 2
Then

NICK *and I were about to be married, and I had this sense that something bad was about to happen. I'd had it before, but everyone thought it was voodoo crap. Then I'd remind them of the time I hadn't wanted to go on the London Underground. What had happened next? Boom – the train blew up due to a terrorist attack. That one small, uneasy feeling was the only reason I'd ever got to see my family again.*

To be fair, I'd never believed in that sort of stuff either. I still didn't, but at least I'd learned to trust my gut. Now, after being stuck in this flat with a screaming three-year-old, I was starting to get the jitters. Hayden was in bed by then, thank God, but Nick and his best friend were enjoying their stag night, and neither of them had texted me in hours. That's not to say I was needy – I was just a concerned fiancée. I still didn't dare disturb their last big night.

It was two in the morning by the time I heard scratching at the door. I initially thought it was an intruder trying to break in, mostly because I'd fallen asleep and woken up in a blind panic while not really knowing where I was. But when my brain caught up and I realised I'd left the key in the door, I rushed out of bed to greet the drunks.

Unsurprisingly, my fiancé was hanging off his best friend, his eyes barely open. I loved Nick – he was perfect in every way – but I had to laugh when I saw him like that. Ryan held him up in his strong arms, grinning like an idiot as I stepped back to let them in.

'Kate. Wonderful to see you,' he said with an exaggerated English accent.

There was no fooling me – the staggering suggested he was no gentleman.

'How much has he had?' I asked Ryan.

'Enough that he probably doesn't know where he is. Just as planned.'

'Oh, God help us all.'

Ryan sneered again as he helped my man

through the door. We worked together to get him inside, heaving him onto the bed and slipping off his shoes. I told Ryan to let me be alone with Nick for a second and that he could go help himself to water and a seat if he liked. As soon as he left, I found a bucket and placed it beside the bed, then rolled Nick onto his side. He groaned groggily, but he was still a sight to behold. I always said he looked like a young Russell Crowe, and others had agreed. Some with more lust than I was comfortable with.

Still, I loved that he was mine. We'd met online, which was supposed to be taboo, but it was the best date I ever had. He took me to the aquarium, and then we went dancing, and we finished off with some of the best Mexican food I'd ever had. I'd immediately told my mum I was going to marry this man. She'd sneered, but we were actually making it happen.

Nick was my soulmate.

When he began snoozing, I decided it was safe to leave him. Seeing he still had water by the bed, I turned the light off and crept out of the room. Most women would be upset that he'd come home in such a state. But me?

I was just glad he had fun.

. . .

I MADE the biggest mistake of my life that night.

Ryan was sitting on the sofa when I returned to the living room, sitting spread-legged and nursing a glass of water between his legs. His head was knocked back, the five o'clock shadow announcing itself on his dark neck. I tried not to disturb him, but I was worried he'd fallen asleep, and I was almost certain he'd tip that water all over the furniture. I reached for it, and the moment my hand touched the glass, he woke up.

'Oi, I need that,' he said with a smile.

'Sorry.' I laughed and slumped next to him, making sure my robe sash was tied. I exhaled as my back hit the plush cushion, then joined him in staring up at the ceiling. We often had moments like these – just taking a moment to let life slow down – and it was always comforting.

'Long day?' Ryan asked.

'Not really. I mean, Hayden has been a handful, and I've been worried about Nick, but everything has gone pretty smoothly. What did that man of mine get up to, anyway? Anything I need to be worried about?'

'A gentleman never tells.'

'I don't think that applies to this situation.'

'Fine, but I won't spill. You'll have to ask him.'

I smiled and kept my head back, studying the specks of paint on the ceiling. It was mostly curiosity that had me asking. The truth was, I trusted Nick with every fibre of my being. He wouldn't betray me if his life depended on it.

'Aren't you drunk?' I asked Ryan.

'No, love. Tonight was more about pouring drinks down the groom's throat.'

'Yeah, thanks for that. I'll probably be mopping up sick tomorrow.'

'You lucky gal.'

'Shut up.' I hit him playfully. 'What time are you leaving?'

Ryan rolled his head to one side and looked right at me. I did the same to him. He was frowning, poking out his bottom lip as he imitated a petulant child. 'Are you going to make me walk home alone at this time of night? It's about an hour away.'

'You can stay on the sofa,' I said. 'But kick your shoes off.'

'Trying to get my clothes off already, are you?'

I smiled and shook my head. Ryan had always had a flirty nature. We'd gone on a date once or twice, but that was some years ago. We'd kissed from time to time, then mutually agreed that we were more like friends. At least, I thought it was mutual, but I'll never know.

There was a long period of time between that and the day we started hanging out platonically. When the time came to start dating again, I'd set up an online profile, met Nick, and fell in love. I didn't realise they were friends until later.

'If I wanted your clothes off, I'd have it done,' I said.

'Cocky.'

'It's true. You know it, I know it.'

'Then what are you waiting for?'

I crooked an eyebrow and made the brutal mistake of glancing at his lips. I almost got away with it, but then I saw him looking at mine. Our eyes met, but I felt nothing. No excitement, no enticement, no nothing.

Until he leaned over and tried to kiss me.

I snapped back for a second, his lips grazing mine. Ryan's face turned a slight shade of red, and I couldn't get a word out while trying to figure out this new bolt of electricity coursing through me. Regretting it before it even happened, I leaned in for a real kiss – this one lasting five to ten seconds. My heart was racing as his hand slid onto my knee, and *despite the erotic fantasy appealing to me for a millisecond, it had to end right there.*

'No,' I said, pulling away a second time. 'Sorry, that was a mistake.'

Ryan nodded and looked hurt, but his hand didn't move. I pointed at it and asked him to take it off, but he took a little too long doing it. When I physically removed it from my leg, he fought back for an instant, registered the discomfort in my eyes, then finally let go.

'That was bad,' he said.

'Yes, it was.'

'But the good kind of bad?'

'Maybe if I were single...'

'But you're not.'

'Right.'

The room grew uncomfortably silent. Nick stirred in the next room, and I rushed to my feet to make sure he hadn't just seen what happened. Whether or not I would tell him about it was something Ryan and I would have to discuss later. For now, I pushed the bedroom door open very slightly and saw Nick had simply rolled over in bed.

Breathing a sigh of relief, I returned to the living room for the last time. Ryan was lying on the sofa then, his belt uncoiled from his waist and the button of his jeans undone. It looked somewhat suggestive, but maybe that was the shame talking. When Ryan craned his neck, he looked me up and down, drawing attention to the fact my robe had come undone. I quickly folded it over and stood there with a pounding heart, terrified about what had almost happened.

'Goodnight' was all I could manage to say.

'Goodnight,' Ryan said back, then rolled over.

Consumed by guilt and regret, I turned off the light and went back into my bedroom, slipping in beside Nick and wondering what the hell I'd just done to him. Would my secret get out, or did I have to tell him myself? The latter, probably.

I just hoped I could do it on my own terms.

RYAN WAS ALREADY GONE *when I woke up the next day. It surprised me because he'd always been a heavy sleeper, and I was up at sunrise to prepare the day for Hayden. Even at the age of three, our son liked to sleep in as long as possible. That wouldn't have been a problem except, once he was up, he wasn't going back down until bedtime. It left very little time for living, so it was a good thing I didn't work, as Nick had a decent career as a doctor.*

As usual, my day began by opening all the curtains and letting the British sunlight pour in through the windows. The flat looked totally different in the day, so bright it looked like some shoddy TV set for Heaven itself. I let in a little breeze and started making meals for the day, including some chicken and rice for Nick to take to work. If he decided to go, that was.

It was a perfectly normal day in all regards except one. As much as I tried to fight it, my mind rebelled and flashed images of my late-night betrayal into my brain. It made me sick to think what I'd done to Nick and even sicker to consider what might have happened if I hadn't stopped it. Ryan was attractive, but that didn't give us a right to stab anyone in the back.

When the bacon hit the pan with a satisfying hiss, a waft of smell filled the kitchen. It must have reached the bedroom because Nick was up and walking around before the meat even needed flipping. He stayed in his boxer shorts and a plain white tee that hugged his impressive frame. He was no bodybuilder, but he obviously took care of himself. Most people would think he worked day and night to look like that – all it really took was a few rowing sessions here or there. There was nothing Nick loved more than being out on the Thames.

Except for me and his son.

I shuddered with shame as he came over and kissed me, rubbing his eyes with the heels of his hands as he made coffee. Without asking, he poured me a cup and put it in front of me. This was typical of him – looking out for me even when his head was pounding.

'Good night?' I asked.

'The best. So far, anyway.'

'Ooh, got something good coming up?'

'Our wedding night, and every night that follows it.'

A smile escaped my lips, but I bit it back with guilt once more.

'Is Hayden up?' Nick asked.

'Not yet. And I'd like to keep it that way.'

'Yes, ma'am.'

We ate the bacon and eggs in silence, leaving some aside for our son whenever he decided to wake up. Nick admired the view, squinting as the morning light kissed his face. He chewed, looking deep in thought as he wolfed down the sustenance he needed to make it through the day. It occurred to me I could tell him about my infidelity right then.

There was a slim chance he would take it relatively well, appreciate that sometimes bad things happened for no reason, then make me promise to never do it again. And I'd make that promise – this was the only mistake I'd ever make, especially if it threatened our marriage.

'Nick,' I said softly. 'I have something to tell you.'

But Nick didn't move. He just carried on eating and staring out the window.

'What's that?' he asked.

This was my golden opportunity. The fork in the road that could either ensure the survival of our upcoming wedding or obliterate it altogether. I thought of Hayden in the next room and how broken he would feel if his mum and dad split up. Call me selfish – I'd have agreed with you – but I just couldn't bring myself to take that risk.

'I forgot to pay the electric bill,' I said.

'That's no problem.' Nick swallowed and reached for his coffee. 'I'll take care of it.'

Chapter 3
Now

By the time our prize is processed – and believe me when I say I have no idea what led me to win this thing – a few days have passed. Hayden is officially out of school for the Christmas holidays, and Sean is off work. There's nothing to do but pack, start driving overnight, and make it into Scotland in the late morning.

I'm not sure what any of us expected from Scotland. I've never been, and neither has Sean. If you're into green scenery and some rough roads, this is the place for you. See, I've always been a city girl, and it's a hard adjustment, but a few muddy puddles and a cold blast of air isn't going to change that. I still want nothing to do with this stupid holiday season.

The prize distributor instructed us to meet him at a farm just outside of the woods. Sean handled most of the planning, while I got to packing for the three of us. I always trust him, and that was the right thing to do – he always knows how to handle things.

We pull up outside a small, white cottage surrounded by fields. Ahead of us, an awe-inspiring forest ranges as far as our field of view will reach. The trees are tall and magnificent, but there isn't so much as a dirt path between them and us. That's why we're here, Sean says as he gets out of the car and lets in the smell.

This is enough to make Hayden stir.

'It stinks of poo,' he says.

It's not like I'm going to disagree, but we are on the animals' land. Moreover, the cottage nearby has tracks leading around the side, with a large, open barn at the end of it. It's immediately obvious this is farmland, which tells me we're in the right place.

'Where's Sean gone?' Hayden asks from the back seat of our rental car.

'We're supposed to meet some people here,' I say, watching Sean knock on the door. It springs open, and he's invited inside, leaving us isolated in the dirt, bang in the middle of nowhere. 'They're going to pack us into a jeep, and then we're going into the woods.'

'Why don't we just drive there?'

'Part of the package, I suppose. This car will never make it anyway.'

'Why not?'

I explain that our holiday venue is deep in the woods and that it's all through soggy dirt and deep bogs. Without a jeep and a skilled driver to take us through it, we might as well head back to London. This should bother me, but I quite like the isolation. Like I said, the further we can get from all the seasonal crap, the better.

Sean returns a few minutes later with a tall, skinny man dressed in filthy navy dungarees. He peers over at our car and waves with a goofy smile. I wave back, but Hayden just sinks back in his seat and huffs loud enough for the whole world to hear.

'What's wrong?' I ask.

'My friends are all at home with their families.'

'You're with yours.'

'But Dad isn't here.'

I don't know what to say, so I just lean back and take his hand, then continue to watch Sean. The man is pointing up at the trees as if to guide him. For a minute, it looks like he's not going to take us up there, but then he leaves Sean alone and disappears behind the building.

Sean returns to us.

'This is it,' he says. 'He's going to get the jeep. We just need to have our things ready.'

'What about our car?'

'I'll take it around the side when we're unloaded.'

As soon as I step out of the car, a rush of freezing December wind hits me in the face. It takes my breath away, sweeping my hair all over the place. I pull some from my mouth and pay no attention to the farm smell, tell Hayden to stay put, then start moving the bags with Sean at my side. As we scramble to clear the luggage from the boot, he smiles at me. I've never seen anything so assuring in all my life, and suddenly, it's so clear.

We badly need this break.

THE MAN OFFERS a grubby hand and introduces himself as Malcolm. I shake it and try not to let it show that germs freak me the hell out. He's turning around before I get a chance to embarrass myself like that, and he quickly loads our luggage into the mud-coated jeep. It rocks as our suitcases pile in the back, which tells me the suspension is either excellent or terrible.

'It might get a little crowded during the ride,' he says, still heaving the bags as oo's and ahh's punctuate his Scottish accent. I recognise his voice from when I called to arrange the trip. 'Ma dog sometimes rides with me, so there's fur in the back. You're not allergic, are ye? I can leave her in the house if ye are.'

'Nobody is allergic,' Sean says, smiling and holding the door open for me.

I stand back and usher Hayden inside, whispering not to be rude as he pulls a face at the blanket in the back. It's webbed with old, white dog fur that's coming up in clumps. Without too much protest, he clambers in and bites his tongue. A moment later, Sean and Malcolm join us, taking the front seats as we set off into the woods.

It feels like we're heading into the great beyond. The trees are too thick to let the sunlight in, so the jeep bounces and rocks into darkness, navigating the muddy, rocky terrain with expert precision as we weave between the trunks. Hayden keeps knocking into me, so I put my arm around him and hold him close. He doesn't need to tell me he's scared – I can feel it in his trembling hands. It only makes me hold him closer.

'Are you okay back there?' Sean asks.

'We're fine,' I tell him, turning my attention to Malcolm. 'How far is it?'

'By car? About thirty minutes, unless we run inta some mud. Happens a lot around here. And trust me, ye don't want that. Ye have to hike through these woods, it's unlikely ye'll get out without a good sense of direction. Even if ye do, it's at least three or four hours.'

I shoot a look at Sean, who catches it in the vanity mirror and smiles.

'She's probably wondering how we're getting back,' he tells Malcolm.

Malcolm lets out a deep belly laugh. 'I'm coming ta get ye when it's time to leave.'

'So we're stuck up here?' I ask. 'What if something happens?'

'Well, I don't know if they have a phone, but ye'll have neighbours up there. Maybe they can call me, although I don't think ye'll get a very good reception. Like I said, nobody around here for miles. Except them folks, anyhow.'

I lean forward and place a hand on his seat. 'I thought we were supposed to be alone?'

'Aye, ye will be. Except for them.'

'Great.'

Sean laughs softly from the front, mostly just to rescue the situation. It's not intentional, but I'm coming across as rude. I really was hoping to be completely secluded during this trip. We don't need to see neighbours putting up Christmas decorations as a reminder.

'Something a matter?' Malcolm asks.

'She just wanted to get away from the festivities,' Sean says. 'They had a bad experience one year, and now it's just awful by association.'

'Ah, ye shouldn't worry. Yer neighbours hate Christmas, too.'

I suppose that makes me feel a little better, so I sit back with a polite smile and put my arm back around Hayden, who hugs me tight. As we dive deeper into the forest, it gets darker and rougher. We hold on tight to each other while I try telling myself this is going to be fine. If we have some kind of accident and urgently need to contact the outside world, at least there are people nearby to help with that. Malcolm said the reception is terrible, but maybe they have a landline. The internet. A fax machine. *Something.*

'Ye folks pay much for this trip, if ye don't mind me asking?' Malcolm says.

'We won it from some competition,' Sean informs him.

'Oh aye. In a magazine or something?'

'Actually, I'm not sure. Kate?'

All I can do is shrug, but when I realise neither of the men up front can see it, I opt for vocals instead. 'To be honest, I do a lot of competitions. Magazines, websites, TV game shows. It's not like we need the money, but I always thought it'd be nice to win something.' I pause for thought. 'If you didn't think we paid, how was this trip arranged with you?'

'I usually get a phone call from the agent, but this time, someone else rang me up. Asked if I could get ye in at short notice. Not that I deal with the bookings, but anyone who visits sort of needs to go through me.'

'Sounds like it can be annoying?'

'Not really. I get ta treat me wife with the money it gives.'

Sean smiles at him, and then I turn my attention to the woods outside. It really is starting to feel like we're heading into complete blackness, with branches whipping at the windows like furious snakes. Only thin ripples of light break through the thin gaps in the leaves above, slicing through the air like thin rain. I wonder how much farther it is and pray that, during our stay, none of us needs to get back into town.

MY BACK IS sore from being tossed around in the jeep, so I'm quick to make my escape as soon as we reach our destination. The very first thing that happens is as crappy as it can get – my foot plunges right into a thick, pungent puddle, seizing my shoe as I try to wiggle free. Hayden bursts into laughter, but as sadistic as he can sometimes be, he's equally kind in nature. He comes to my rescue, beating Sean and Malcolm to it by seconds.

When I'm finally liberated from the mud, I walk around to the back and look at the two single-storey cottages in the clearing. They're pretty much identical, though the neighbours' is a sickly yellow. The kind of sunrise colour only an elderly person might choose. Ours, on the other hand, has flaking white paint with a nicely tiled roof, lots of windows, and a small portion of wall made from logs, presumably an extension. Other than those details, it's symmetrical to the nearby cottage and only a short walk away.

'Go see them if ye need a hand,' Malcolm says, unloading the car. 'I'll be up here a week from now, so try ta be ready. And don't even think about walking downhill, especially at night. Trust me, a muddy boot will be the last of ye worries.'

Sean pays him a tip – generous as ever, while I stand there like a useless wench, staring at our accommodation. It looks nice and cosy, and I'm pleased to see there's not a Christmas decoration in sight. I'm starting to think we could get away with this – that I won't have to think of Nick's death for a second, much less the fact his murderer is still out there somewhere. He was identified on the night by yours truly but, sadly, never apprehended.

There I go, ruining it for myself again. I don't know if it's just that chilling thought or the fact we're in the middle of nowhere and unable to get any kind of help even if we need it. There's still a cold shudder running through me, and I don't like the feeling I'm having.

'Something wrong?' Sean asks.

I watch Hayden with my shoulders slouching, then feel that shiver again. I attempt to shake it off, trying my best to start fresh and have the first good holiday season in years. There will be no tears, no breakdowns, and absolutely no depression. It's just me, Sean, and my son.

'I'm fine,' I say. 'Come on, let's enjoy ourselves for once.'

Chapter 4
Then

*T*HE FIRST WEEKEND *after my kiss with Ryan, Nick and I took Hayden to the Natural History Museum. We'd been talking about how bad it was that we were both born Londoners and neither of us had been. The fact that it was a museum implied it might not be perfect for an active three-year-old, so we had a backup plan to just go for ice cream instead.*

As usual, Nick didn't hesitate to take control of the baby bag, slinging it onto his back while unfolding the pushchair for Hayden. Our son could walk just fine, but he got tired easily, and this might have ended up being a long day. We had no idea.

There was no queue time at all. Plenty of people walked up the long, wide path outside to approach the main hall, and we were inside quicker than expected. Nick, charitable as ever, slipped a twenty-pound note into the charity donation and didn't even stick around to receive thanks for it. That was Nick all over – kind and generous.

It made me sick with guilt.

The museum's main hall was a sight to behold. A grand staircase waited at the far end, while massive pillars separated the many wings. The crowd was large and buzzing, but my attention was fixed on Hayden, who was jerking his finger up at the ceiling from his pushchair. I followed his finger and was awed to see an enormous skeleton suspended from the ceiling.

'Skeleton!' he yelled excitedly.

'That's right,' I said. 'I wonder what it's of.'

'It's a blue whale,' Nick said.

I turned to look at him, awaiting an explanation for how he'd acquired his knowledge.

'I saw it online,' he said.

Before we ventured any deeper, Nick needed a quick toilet break. I waited outside with Hayden, kneeling by his pushchair and asking him what he'd like to see first. As people breezed past and kept knocking me – some with apologies, some without – I explained the many attractions that awaited us.

The excitement in his eyes was nothing short of magical, but there was also something else. Something darker.

'What's wrong?' I asked.

'Mummy, why did you kiss Ryan?'

My heart almost dropped into my stomach. I glanced around to make sure Nick wasn't back from the toilets, then shuffled closer to him, lowering my voice as much as I could over the activity of the museum. How stupid of us to come on a Saturday.

'What are you talking about?' I asked, hoping he'd misspoken or I'd misheard.

'You kissed him on the sofa.'

'Why weren't you in bed?'

'I couldn't sleep.'

It mortified me that not only did I kiss Nick's best friend, but my three-year-old son had witnessed it. It broke my heart to realise how confused he must be, but it was worse than that. Now I had to lie to him just to cover my tracks. I felt like a complete rat.

'It was just a friendly kiss on the cheek,' I explained.

Hayden touched his lips, correcting me, stubborn in what he'd seen.

'No, it was on the cheek. It was dark, and you

saw it wrong.' I took another glance towards the toilets, where a huge stream of people fought over who got to go and relieve themselves first. Nick was nowhere in sight, but he could easily be nearby. 'Listen, you can't tell Daddy about it, okay? He'll think I did something bad, and then we can't be a family any more.'

Watching Hayden's face scrunch up with a mixture of confusion and sadness was one of the worst things I'd ever had to see. I loved my son more than anything else in the world and Nick just as much. Why did I have to make that dumb mistake, and how on earth was I supposed to hide it forever? It didn't seem doable, even if I could live with the guilt.

'Everything okay here?'

Nick's voice made me startle so hard I almost lost my balance. I stood up and smiled at him, then kissed him on the lips to distract him. If he looked down and saw Hayden's face, he might've had more questions.

'It's all good. Hayden was just asking about the dinosaurs.' I turned back to our son, asking if he wanted to go and see some dinosaur bones. The diversion worked, his face lighting up as a child's always should, and I reached for the pushchair handles as fast as possible, just to steer him away from Nick's line of sight.

But Nick intercepted, offering to take the duty away from me like he always did. He was such a good man, and it only made me feel worse about the horrible thing I'd done. Surely, I had to tell him eventually.

I just couldn't bring myself to do it.

It WAS ONLY two more days until our wedding, and my phone was blowing up. As Nick and I sat in a Starbucks and went over the final details, I left it to one side and tried not to be distracted by the constant ringing. Nick suggested I take five minutes to enjoy my latte and red velvet cake, and maybe he was right – the stress had been bogging me down for some time.

I sat back, cut off a small slice of cake with the fork, and enjoyed the sweet treat. The cream was thick and flavoursome, and the coffee to chase it was hot and alerting. This was heaven, but checking my phone sent me crashing back to earth.

There were two messages from my mother, both asking the same question twice: could she come and see me the day before I got married? Of course she could – she was my maid of honour since I had very few female friends to speak of. She always was a persistent woman, but she meant well. Which is to say I trusted her to take care of things. I typed out a reply, telling her we would go out for food and enjoy ourselves, then hit Send.

It was the other messages that shook me.

I had four texts from Ryan, each growing increasingly impatient. The first asked if I wanted to meet him in private, while the following two messages started hinting at what might happen if I did. The timestamp on the fourth showed he'd waited a little over an hour before he finally lost control and told me off for not having replied. I glanced up at Nick to see if he could read my reaction, but thankfully, he was focused on the seating plan in front of him.

My thumbs danced around the phone, telling him it was a mistake and that we couldn't take it any further. I tried to phrase it in a way that Nick wouldn't know what it meant if he happened to look at my inbox one day – he never did, but accidents could always happen.

However, I was still typing when the picture came through.

Ryan had undressed himself and taken a close-

up shot of his... well, I'm too much of a lady to use the correct term, but let's just say I now know he's circumcised. My hands went shaky. I pulled the phone to my chest as my face grew steaming hot. I suddenly felt sick to the point that coffee and cake didn't interest me.

It got worse when Nick looked up.

'Sweetheart, you're all red. Are you all right?'

'Yes,' I stumbled. 'Slight complication with my wedding dress.'

'Want me to take a look at it?'

'You can't,' I snapped. 'It's bad luck.'

'Well, if you change your mind...'

He went back to studying the seating plan, and I forced myself into looking at my phone again. I squinted a little as I typed because I didn't want to see that picture ever again. My hands cooked up a reply before my brain could even make sure it was a good idea:

Stop messaging me. We're not an item.

As soon as the message sent, I deleted all exchanges between the two of us and put my phone in my pocket. It immediately buzzed against my leg, once, twice, then a third time within a single minute. A morbid part of me was curious about what he might have written back, but it would have to wait. I was supposed to be enjoying the final prep for my wedding.

'I think that's perfect,' Nick said, turning the book around for me to see.

There were circles everywhere, with stick-on names dotted around them to show where everyone would be seated. I tried my best to concentrate as I examined the layout, nodding with approval. I wish I'd not looked, however, because then I realised something that made me so uncomfortable I was ready to bring the red velvet cake right back up.

Ryan would be sitting at our table.

LATER THAT NIGHT, Nick arranged for a few of us to have dinner in our flat. We'd both been so busy with the wedding planning lately, and Hayden was having a tough time with his new sleep schedule, so we spent a fortune on Chinese food and shared it around the table.

The food was amazing, if a bit more oily than I'd have liked, but it was hard to enjoy with present company. I loved everyone around the table, which consisted of two couples we'd gone to college with, plus Ryan, who conveniently sat himself next to me. I could have sworn his hand brushed my leg under the table a couple of times, so I kept making excuses to go to the kitchen. This way, I could swig some wine and take a breather.

The last time I did it was a big mistake.

I was at the sink, letting a warm red wine trickle down my throat, when the swinging door creaked open. The reflection in the window showed Ryan sneaking up behind me, so I turned and tried to play nice. But I didn't get to utter a word because his hands were already on my hips as he moved in for an aggressive kiss.

Dropping the wine glass into the dishwater, I tried to force his hands off me, but he was too strong. His breath was hot and smelled like beer, which he'd been using to wash down the food. I kept moving my head, frantically trying to evade the kiss while he persisted.

'Stop it!' I snapped.

Ryan didn't stop, but he did slow down. His hands remained on my hips, but at least he stopped trying to kiss me. I just wish I could bring myself to look him in the eye.

'What, so you thought you could kiss me once and then discard me like a used tissue?'

'It was a mistake, Ryan. I thought that was clear.'

'But mistakes can be fun. Let's keep making them.'

'No.' I shook my head, closing my eyes tight. 'It won't happen again. Now, get off.'

I tried to break free and walk around him, but he shoved me so hard into the kitchen worktop that a shot of pain rippled up my back. I let out a short cry and heard the dining room go dead silent. Ryan paused, holding me in place while we waited to see what would happen.

The whole time, I was praying for someone to come in.

They didn't.

'Everything okay in there?' Nick's voice sounded from the next room.

'It's all good,' Ryan yelled back. 'Kate just stubbed her toe.'

A pause. Then: 'Kate?'

The way Ryan looked at me then, I wouldn't dare drop him in it. It was bad enough he was being this rough with me, but knowing he could easily tell Nick about the kiss and ruin my marriage? No, I had to play along with it.

'I'm fine,' I called.

The mutterings recommenced around the table, and Ryan got back to trying to smooch with me. I put all my effort into pushing him off me and, surprisingly, succeeded. My freedom lasted all of two seconds before he rushed at me again, harder this time. Before I knew it, I was pulling my shoulder back to deliver a slap so hard that its echo sang around the kitchen.

Ryan stopped dead in his tracks, touching a hand to his pink cheek.

'I've warned you,' I said. 'There's nothing between us.'

Then something happened that I never thought I would see. Ryan's usually kind eyes turned cold, his upper lip curving into an animalistic snarl. His leg twitched like he wanted to run at me. His free hand clenched into a fist. It was hard to breathe, even harder to move.

There was no telling what he would do if I tried.

'Just so you understand,' he said with a heat-filled growl, 'you and I are going to have one hell of a time together in the bedroom. It's the least you owe me after all this time of being a tease. It might not be tonight or tomorrow, but it's going to happen. And if you refuse me again, I'll tell Nick all about our little game of tonsil tennis. Are we clear?'

He didn't even wait for an answer – he simply snagged the bottle of wine I'd been drinking and went back into the dining room as if nothing had happened. Alone and frightened in my own kitchen, I tried as hard as I could to hold back the tears.

I lasted all of five seconds.

Chapter 5
Now

HAYDEN UNLOCKS the door ahead of us and bursts into the cottage before we can tell him more. An eight-year-old's energy is hard to deal with, especially when you're travelling, so we just let him enjoy his freedom. Besides, it doesn't look as though there's any nearby danger.

I've grabbed a suitcase and am hauling it in with a bear grip as the wheels won't spin in this boggy terrain. I set it down inside the door and let my eyes roam over the cottage's interior. It has an old, rustic feel, with soft tree lights wrapped around the oak beams. There are pillars in the middle of the room and an old fireplace with a small wooden log store right beside it. There's a seating area with deep sofas and a kitchen to die for.

For the first time in years, I've made the right choice.

'You going to leave me standing in the door-way?' Sean asks behind me.

'Sorry,' I laugh, moving into the expanse. Hayden is at the far back, where a deceptively long corridor leads to three different rooms. A bathroom and two bedrooms, I expect, although the cottage didn't look big enough for it from the outside. 'There's just two more bags.'

'I'll get them. You go and put your feet up.'

'Nope. One each, and that's final.'

Sean holds up his hands in mock surrender, and then we return outside. I stop briefly in the clearing to look up at the sky. With all the light blocked out by the tall surrounding trees, along with the grey curdling of the clouds above, it feels like we're in some sort of dark pit. Most people would hate this, but the solitude feels comforting to me. In fact, the excitement of being somewhere new is giving me goosebumps. The good kind.

Startling me out of my trance, Sean buzzes past me and makes a solid Road Runner impersonation, beep-beeping me out of his path. It makes me giggle as I hurry for the last remaining suitcase that's currently sitting in a pool of mud. It doesn't bother me – suitcases are made for poor treatment. It's the contents that really matter.

I see that Sean has taken the food supplies and left me with just the lighter case, and I smile before carrying it back in. When I set it down with all the others, Sean is already putting the kettle on. It gurgles and bubbles as he drops teabags into some mugs. When the water settles and the kettle spews out the last of its steam, the cottage becomes eerily quiet.

It's unsettling.

'Hayden?' I call, wondering what he's up to. 'Do you need a snack?'

Silence.

Sean turns to me, then abandons what he's doing as we both storm up the corridor, splitting into different rooms in a chaotic but organised search for my son. My blood is running cold when I find the room empty, and as I meet a confused-looking Sean in the hallway, we check the final room. The small bathroom is empty.

Hayden is gone.

Panic rises to my thumping chest as we both run outside. Sweat forms on my brow, and I'm about to call his name before I hear voices. Sean opens his mouth to yell, but I shush him and concentrate on listening, then follow the sound around to the side, within the gap between the two cottages. I find what I want straight away.

Hayden is there, his hands stuffed in his pockets, as a big, older man stands there holding a hosepipe. He looks to be in his mid-sixties, with white, receding hair and a neatly trimmed beard that colour-matches the top of his head. He's dressed in a wool coat that looks too big in this surprising forest warmth. When he sees us, he turns to smile at me.

I get the sense he's not dangerous.

'Are you this boy's mother?' he asks.

The first thing I pick up on is his English accent. I don't know why it surprises me, but I half expected him to be Scottish. Sean and I head towards them. Hayden steps back into Sean's arms, almost as if he's scared. But his expression is more shy than frightened.

'Sorry if he's bothering you,' I say. 'He's a curious kid, you know?'

'It's no bother at all. In fact, he's a very polite young boy. Came over and asked if I needed any help with the gardening.' The man gestures a hand towards the flower bed under his window, and now the hosepipe makes sense. 'Are you moving in or just visiting?'

'Just spending a few days here over Christmas.' Sean extends a hand, and the man takes it before reaching for mine. 'Sean Edwards, and this is my girlfriend, Kate. You've already met young Hayden.'

'Frank,' the man says, taking my hand in his warm palm. 'You from England?'

'Yes, London,' I tell him.

'I spent a little time in London when I was younger. Never could live with the busyness.'

'It's better if you grew up around it. Easy to adjust then.'

'True. But now we live up here. Me and the wife. Nice and quiet, see.'

Sean seems to read into that hint, excusing ourselves from the intrusion. Meanwhile, I'm distracted by how similar their cottage is to ours. I also can't stop thinking about how it might feel to live up here. The distance from civilisation might be good for a few days, but I can imagine it being lonely up here. Almost dangerously so, for those who get depressed easily.

'Don't go worrying yourselves about being rude

or anything,' Frank says. 'My wife and I were just about to eat. We have plenty of food to go around and a lovely patio out of the mud around the back. You're welcome to join us.'

I look to Sean, who shrugs, then says, 'That would be nice.'

'Great. Always good to know your neighbours. Now, go and unpack, then come find us in, say' – Frank glances at his watch – 'twenty minutes?'

'Sounds good to us.'

Before I can utter a word of protest, Sean touches my shoulder and encourages us inside. I didn't plan on spending our alone time with anyone, but our neighbour seems like a lovely man, and it might be a nice distraction from the exhaustion that's been wearing me down.

I smile and raise a hand to wave, and then we head inside our own cottage to unpack.

'This could be nice,' Sean says when we're back inside.

'Yes,' I say. 'This is a good start.'

It's surprising that I feel perfectly comfortable on someone else's property. It helps that the gazebo is gorgeous. It's solid wood, with a nice, tiled roof and plenty of lanterns to make it feel warmer than it probably is. We're sitting at a large, traditional picnic bench with a wide range of juicy meats and fresh vegetables that were apparently grown right here.

Frank's wife is nice, too. Her name is Jeanie, and she's just as friendly as Frank. Maybe even more so, despite initially looking miserable. I thought she was going to complain that there was a kid staying next door to her peaceful retreat, but she softened immediately. She's a small but lively woman, considering she's treading somewhere between sixty and seventy. She looks exactly like Frank's female counterpart, white-haired and approachable.

'So, what brings you to Deepwood?' she asks, offering a bowl of wine-cooked chicken.

I take it with a grin and start loading Hayden's plate, then my own. 'I won a competition.'

'I heard something about the owners doing that,' Frank says. 'It's a nice idea.'

'Doesn't it bother you to keep having new people arrive?' I ask.

'Not at all. We get to meet all different sorts of folk. Like your good selves.'

Another smile makes its way to my lips. I pass

the bowl and start putting potato wedges and salad onto our plates. The smell of all this food is making my mouth water. Hayden and Sean must be hungry, too, as they're eating without a single word. It looks like it's down to me to be the conversationalist.

'I noticed you don't have any Christmas decorations up,' I say. 'Is that a religious thing?'

'Not at all,' Jeanie explains. 'We just never really liked this time of year.'

'Mind if I ask why?'

'It's just too...' Jeanie seems to be struggling, so Frank steps in to save her.

'Commercial?'

Jeanie snaps her fingers. 'That's it.'

I can't help but agree because even if my husband wasn't murdered on Christmas Day, I still might not be overly fond of December. It's too much of a show, trying to force festive foods down our throats and convince us to buy stuff for people who already have enough. This year is different in many ways, however. Not only are we away from all that, but Hayden can receive his brand-new PlayStation as soon as we return home. Until then, there are a bunch of smaller presents to keep him happy on the big day.

We all sink into mindless chatter, more about the weather and the types of people who frequently use the cottage. Hayden has finished his food, and his leg is anxiously bobbing up and down. I tell him he can go play, as long as he doesn't wander too far. He doesn't hesitate to launch himself off the bench like a rocket and go running into the trees.

We're all laughing at his energy. Sean downs his beer and then asks the serious question.

'Do you guys happen to have a phone in case of emergencies?'

Frank shakes his head and dabs his mouth with a napkin. 'Sorry, but we did away with all those modern conveniences. Sort of defeats the point of living out in the sticks. I bet you have mobile phones, but we hear the signal isn't great out here.'

I set down my fork and dive into my pocket for my phone. I'm not sure why it hasn't occurred to me to check – I just took Malcolm at his word and assumed there was no reception. The empty bar at the top of the screen proves he was right. To be honest, it might be nice to assure us that Hayden could get medical help if he needed it, but I still like being out here.

As long as nothing goes horribly wrong.

. . .

TIME FLIES BY. Somehow, an afternoon wind finds its way through the clearing and makes me shiver. My maternal instincts make me wonder if Hayden is warm enough. I turn to ask him and then remember he's gone to play. How long ago was that now? Thirty minutes? An hour?

'Can you excuse me?' I say, getting up and putting a hand on Sean's shoulder.

'You okay?'

'Fine. I'm going to look for Hayden. You enjoy your beers.'

I feel like the neighbours are watching me – perhaps even thinking I'm rude for abandoning them – but I don't care that much. Hayden's safety is the most important thing in the world to me, and although I'm not too strict of a parent, he knows better than to disappear.

That's why it's so worrying that he hasn't checked in.

I head in the direction he'd run in not too long ago, traipsing through thick weeds that seem to claw for my legs. I'm glad I decided to wear jeans because the foliage would probably be tearing my skin up by now. When I reach a darker section of the woods, I turn around and realise the cottages are no longer in sight. Did Hayden come this far? Is he lost?

'Hayden!' I call, calmly at first, then more alarmed when his voice doesn't echo back.

I pick a direction and stick to it, calling his name over and over. I'm met with dead silence, save for the fleeing of birds from the trees. That fluttering sends cold fear down my spine as the forest simmers into haunting tranquillity. I stand and look around, panic starting to set in as I realise that I'm not the only one who's lost.

Because my son might be, too.

Chapter 6
Sean

SEAN IS HALFWAY between beer sips when he hears Kate calling. There's a brief moment of hesitation, when the message is being sent to his brain and assessed. It's like he can't believe something bad could possibly happen out in the middle of nowhere.

He quickly decides that's not true.

He doesn't so much as glance at Frank and Jeanie, but he does hear them rush to their feet as he dashes off the patio and into the forest. Kate's desperate yells are filled with anguish and despair, which makes the hairs on his nape stand to attention. The hanging branches and wiry vines become an obstacle course that he easily manoeuvres, the primal instinct of being a man pushing him beyond his limits.

'Kate!' he screams, and her voice comes back immediately.

They rush to an embrace, but Sean quickly peels away to check for injuries. She's fine on the outside, but her quivering lip tells the story before she speaks a single word.

Hayden is gone.

'Head back in that direction.' He points. 'Stay at the cottage. I'll find him.'

Kate tries to refuse, but he snaps at her because her feelings are less important than Hayden's well-being. Startled, she blinks in disbelief, pauses for a moment, and then heads off through the same trail of flattened weeds he just ran through.

Alone now, Sean begins to circle the woods, calling out for his son. *Her* son, he must remind himself because as much as he loves the boy, he isn't the dad. Sean has merely adopted the fatherly role, which only tightens the rope around his neck if he doesn't find Hayden.

'Hayden!' he yells at the top of his lungs.

It takes ten whole minutes of searching before he's found. Sean spots him sitting upright on a rock, deep fear set in his eyes. He quickly checks for signs of obvious danger, decides it's okay, then takes careful steps towards him.

'What are you doing out here, mate?'

'Just wanted some peace.'

'Your mum is worried sick.'

'She always is, but I'm okay.'

'Why don't you come back?'

'I just… I want my dad.'

Sean sighs. The weighted conversation comes around every now and then, but the way in which he handles it changes each time. On this occasion, he shifts himself onto the rock, putting an arm loosely around the boy.

'It's hard. I get it. When my dad died, it felt like the whole world had come to an end. It was a heart attack in the middle of the night, so it's not exactly the same, but he was the only person in my entire life I'd ever trusted.'

Hayden doesn't speak, but a soft sob is audible in the forest's silence.

'The thing is, my mum was also alone. She was holding things together, trying to work while raising a kid. Setting aside her own feelings just to make sure I was all right.'

'Were you?' Hayden asks. 'Were you all right?'

'No. I felt how you're probably feeling. But my mother died five years later, and then I grew up a little. I started to realise that she'd been suffering, too. She'd just lost her husband and had to figure out how to be a single parent. Nobody stopped and asked if *she* was okay, and she wouldn't hear it even if they did. All that mattered was my safety.'

Hayden wipes a tear and looks up at him.

'That's how your mum is feeling right now,' Sean says, trying his best not to make it sound like a grilling. 'All she ever worries about is that you're okay. You wandered too far, and now she's back at the cottage, scared to death that she might lose you as well.'

'She won't lose me. I love her.'

'Then do her a kindness and come back to her, okay?'

'Okay.'

Hayden slides off the rock, but Sean is crushed with guilt. Where he tried so hard to convince him that going back was the right thing to do, he completely dismissed the boy's feelings. While Hayden began to walk, Sean called to him. Hayden turned.

'We'll talk about your dad tonight, okay? To get it off your chest.'

'No need,' Hayden says. 'You're not as good as him, but you're *like* my dad.'

Sean smiles, and they return to the cottage together.

Chapter 7
Then

I SHOULD HAVE BEEN *happy on my wedding day, and I would've been were it not for the fact Ryan would be there. My jittery and sleep-deprived mind should have been focused on a whole number of things – the wonderful man I was marrying, my vows, making sure the guests were taken care of. Instead, all I could think of was the mistake I'd made.*

And that Ryan would be standing right up there with Nick.

Our venue was in a beautiful hotel called the Dilly. Nick and I had fallen in love with its elegance and grandeur, instantly marvelling at the high ceilings and the terrace that looked out over London's skyline. It was far out of even our budget, but somehow, we'd made it work. As an added bonus, some of the guests planned to stay over the whole weekend so they could enjoy the swimming pool and incredible food the building was renowned for.

It looked just as good on the day, filling the halls and staircase with the flowers we'd selected after great inspection. My mother extended a hand as we made our way to the hall. Since my father had died long ago, she was the one walking me down the aisle. Don't get me wrong, my mother was an okay person if you didn't take things to heart too easily – I was just thrilled to have somebody there for me. It made me feel less like I was in the spotlight. Anyway, given how tight the corset of my silky dress felt, the fewer people staring, the better.

Looking back, passing out wouldn't have been the worst thing. At least I wouldn't have had to deal with Ryan, much less what came shortly after. At the time, I'd simply been a nervous wreck in every possible way. It was all I could do to focus on the man I was marrying.

The doors opened. The music began, and suddenly, I was on Broadway. Two hundred guests turned to look at me, all grinning like stunned idiots as they obviously had the same positive feelings *about my dress as I'd had. The day was off to a good start.*

How was I supposed to know it wouldn't last?

My mother walked me down the aisle, handing me over to Nick. He wore a dark green suit that would have looked awful on anyone else, but somehow, he donned the unique look with such blasé casualness he could've easily blended in anywhere. I couldn't stop smiling, barely able to believe I was finally marrying the man of my dreams. Our son stood nearby with rings on a pillow. My heart could have melted.

If my eyes hadn't drifted to the man beside him.

Ryan was staring, but he didn't so much as force a smile. As if nobody in the room was looking even remotely in his direction, his eyes had become dark and hollow, staring daggers at me throughout the entire ceremony. It was enough to spoil my mood, making me feel like I was under the spotlight. I tried to fight through it, plastering a false smirk on my face as Hayden tottered over to hand us the rings. Nick and I both kissed him, laughed, and then returned to our vows.

Needless to say, I made a fool of myself. It was the stuttering of words, the inability to form a complete sentence without going back over myself.

Everyone watching laughed, probably assuming I was too smitten to think straight. But if they looked back over the video later, then maybe – just maybe – they would see Ryan mouth the words I swore I was seeing.

'You and me,' his lips seemed to shape. 'Or else.'

Much to my amazement, *I somehow managed to put the Ryan drama behind me. We were celebrating love, after all, and I was thrilled to finally adopt the Bailey surname. Even as the day went on, it still didn't quite feel real, but it didn't hinder my enjoyment of it whatsoever.*

The wedding breakfast was something I'd slowly begun to dread, so you can imagine my discomfort when someone clinked cutlery against a glass and demanded a speech. Everyone laughed and swooned as Nick delivered his, but I was distracted by the fear of what was going to come from Ryan. I wondered if it was even possible that he might say something out of place, then ultimately decided what would be would be.

I became uneasy as soon as he stood up...

And looked directly at me.

'This shouldn't have happened,' he said, and the

whole room froze with their breaths. A smile crept onto his lips, and then his audience began to relax. 'That is, we came from men who hunted for food, used their women for procreation, and lived in caves. Look how far we've come. Nick has bought himself an incredible flat and married the most beautiful girl in London. It seems like an impossibility because Nick is very much still a caveman. Don't believe me? Let me tell you a thing or two about his drinking years.'

I wasn't sure where he was going with his speech, but my friends and family seemed to enjoy it. Ryan even had a little slideshow prepared, showcasing the messes my new husband used to get into during his uni years. Everyone laughed and smiled as he told story after story, none of them quite realising exactly what was happening.

He was trying to embarrass Nick.

Now, I know it's the best man's role to do such a thing, but it felt like he was really going for the jugular. There wasn't a single good thing said about the groom until he was congratulated on "landing himself a hottie", but even that somehow felt like a part of the joke. Everyone's eyes went to me, then glasses were raised, and the breakfast continued.

I didn't dare look at Ryan after that.

As the day went on and the drinks started to flow, my mother began to take more and more care of Hayden. She was set to look after him while we honeymooned in Cornwall, and the cloud of drunkenness started to set in, so it was better he began to slide under her wing. As distanced as she and I had become over the years, I at least knew our son was safe with her.

The sun was setting, and the photographer was done getting the time-sensitive shots. I used this moment to breathe, standing on the terrace and watching the bright orange lights come on all over London. The city was a sight to behold, and I would never get tired of seeing it lit up like that. The fresh evening air was also a comfort, as the wedding dress was slowly suffocating me. I closed my eyes and enjoyed the breeze.

Nothing could have disturbed that perfect moment alone.

'How's that wife of mine?'

I craned my neck to see Nick standing nearby with two champagne flutes in his hands. He offered one to me, we clinked and drank, and then he held my waist from behind and joined me in silence. This was one of the things I loved most about him: he never had to fill an awkward silence.

We both liked peace, so there was no need to ruin it.

Not until he had to, anyway.

'I have a surprise for you,' he whispered in my ear.

I don't know if it was the deep, manly voice or the touch of his lips as they brushed against my earlobe, but I turned to face him, tightening my arms around him and bringing him close.

'Don't tell me you used to be a woman,' I said.

Nick smiled that perfect smile. 'A different surprise.'

'I'm listening.'

'Remember when I said Cornwall is hot this time of year and that you should pack for scorching weather?' His perfect teeth showed, and he was clearly unable to resist hiding his enjoyment at revealing the big secret. 'Well, that was a little trick from yours truly.'

'What do you mean?' I asked innocently.

'Well, we're not exactly going to Cornwall.'

Excitement fluttered within me. 'What did you do?'

'Nothing much. I maybe... booked us a honeymoon in Hawaii.'

'Hawaii!' I screamed a little too loud.

It was the one place in the world I'd always wanted to go, and Nick somehow knew it. I'd had no idea he was even listening to me all those times I rambled on about how nice it looked. I kissed him hard and fully on the lips, absolutely ecstatic about the wonderful surprise. There was literally nothing more he could do to make this day any more perfect.

But my joy was short-lived. No sooner had our lips touched than a panicked shriek erupted from inside. Both our heads spun towards the noise, only to see a bright, yellow blaze bursting across the long table in the Georgian Suite. Our cake was on that table, melting as flames engulfed the very wood it rested on. The Dilly's staff rushed in with fire extinguishers, but they were unable to contain the fire as it spread across the room.

Nick and I didn't stop to think. We both ran for Hayden and my mother, grabbing them just in time for the sprinklers to come on and drench us all. The fire alarm rang throughout the building as everyone hurried for the door, escaping across the road while our wedding day went up in smoke. In that moment, I didn't have time to feel sad or disheartened.

I was too busy praying my friends and family were safe.

73

.   .   .

THE HOTEL ITSELF REMAINED UPRIGHT, the blaze contained to the suite we'd all been celebrating in. Almost two hundred of us were gathered right across the street, some snapping up pictures of the smoke-charred outside wall, while others simply held their loved ones tight.

Nick kept us close, not letting us out of his sight. It was a perfect display of care and affection, which had always made me feel safe. Even then, as fire engines occupied the street and residents of the hotel came to join us in the street, I really didn't feel endangered at all.

When the noise died down, Nick went to investigate and see how the remainder of our big day would pan out. He approached the manager, who we'd overheard being told by the fireman that the cause of the fire was unknown.

Now alone with my mother and son, I lifted my dress slightly and knelt beside Hayden, placing my loving hands gently on his shoulders. I hated the way he was trembling.

'Are you okay?' I asked. 'Are you scared?'
'Yeah.'

'Well, you don't need to be. Daddy has this under control.'

'The poor boy is probably tired,' my mother offered.

I hated to admit it, but she was right. It'd been a long day for him – hell, for all of us – but most of all the three-year-old who'd been inside a burning building. I asked Mum if she could take him back to the hotel, promising to stop by and say goodnight before we turned in. She obliged, and Hayden hugged me tight before going off in her capable hands.

I huffed an exasperated breath, then gathered the train of my wedding dress. It hurt to see passers-by had been treading on it, painting their footprints all over the most expensive dress I'd ever buy. It was hard to do, but I tried to think positively of the experience – I was gathering physical memories on the fabric. Years from now, when I'd find my dress in the wardrobe, I'd spot those footprints and laugh it off because nothing had really changed.

Nick and I had still become husband and wife.

A few of the guests stopped to ask if I was okay, some of my old school friends holding up my dress train. I nodded and turned my attention to Nick, who was coming back with a big smile on his face.

Knowing him, that could have meant absolutely anything.

'Do you want the good news or the bad news?' he yelled above the noise.

All the chattering voices stopped and paid attention, most of them shouting, 'Good!'

'Sorry, you'll have to have the bad news first, otherwise it doesn't sound as good.' He stopped just long enough to let people laugh. 'The bad news is that the hotel will be closed, and our party is not set to continue. The good news is that there's a pub two streets over that have offered to close their doors to customers and will continue to host our celebration in private. So please follow me if you'd like to get drunk and forget about this whole mess.'

Everyone on the street cheered, and I stood there numbly, admiring the man I'd married. Even after a fire at our own wedding, he'd still found a way to make it an amazing night. The street began to clear, and he took my hand. As he did so, I replayed the fireman's voice in my head, announcing they didn't know the cause of the fire. I paused and looked around, finally noticing the one thing that had escaped my notice and piecing it together myself.

Ryan was nowhere to be seen.

Chapter 8
Now

HAYDEN COMES BOUNDING out of the trees and into my arms. Until now, I've been standing with Frank and Jeanie as they tried to comfort me. My nails are chewed to the quick, my heart still pulsing in frantic rhythm. I hold my son close, kissing his head and half-heartedly scolding him for venturing too far from the cottage.

'Sorry, Mum,' he says, holding me tight.

Seconds later, Sean emerges from the trees with a heart-warming smile. Just like I used to do with Nick, I can count on Sean to take care of almost any problem that arises. Maybe that's why I fell in love with him – only a man *like* Nick could help me move on from him.

'It goes without saying, but I'd be careful with your adventures in the forest,' Frank says, patting Sean on the back to approve of his successful return. But he's talking to all of us, letting his eyes wander from me to Hayden – the true target of his advice. 'We had a young girl go missing out here around thirty years ago. Climbing trees, she was.'

'What happened?' Hayden asks curiously.

'She was putting all her weight on a weak branch. It snapped.' Frank makes a noise and uses his hand to demonstrate the break. 'She fell into the mud and couldn't get out because the branch pinned her down. She was stuck there for hours before the rain came. Drowned slowly, probably screaming for her parents.'

'God,' I say. 'So you met the girl who died?'

'No, this was years before we moved in. Malcolm told us the tale.'

'The man who drove us up here?'

'That's right. But he says he saw far worse. There used to be a beast—'

Jeanie slaps him on the arm. 'The young boy doesn't need a horror story.'

'Perhaps he does,' I say, mussing Hayden's hair. 'It might teach him a thing or two.'

Doing our best not to be rude, we thank the neighbours for dinner and offer to return the favour one of these nights. There's no need, they say, but we'll still make the effort regardless. For now, we get inside and thank our lucky stars Hayden came back to us.

That night is one of the best we've had in months, maybe even years. We play Twister, watch DVDs that thankfully have no Christmas connection whatsoever, and share a tube of Pringles. We don't have a care in the world, and why should we?

Christmas no longer exists for us.

Sean offers to put Hayden to bed. I lightly let on that perhaps he's too old to be tucked in, but Hayden seems up for it. He dives into his bedroom while Sean shrugs, laughs, then follows. I don't know what sort of bonding experience those two had in the forest, but it seems to have worked wonders for Hayden's mood. I haven't seen him this happy and excited since before his father's passing. Even if he was too young to remember that fatal day.

It's an opportune moment to uncork a bottle of wine. I choose a red and let it breathe, then pour two glasses. I slump into the dusty sofa and watch a plume of motes launch into the air for the third time today. I don't mind – the old me would have hated getting anything on my expensive clothes, but my own mood has been wound down a little. I'm free for once, simply enjoying life as it's supposed to be enjoyed.

After a few minutes, I realise Sean is taking his time. Sneaking up to the door, I pop my head into Hayden's room and hear them talking about Nick. It always makes me feel guilty that Sean has to hear about the man who came before him, but it's fascinating to see him take it in with such grace. He truly is a remarkable man.

And I'll cherish him forever.

By the time Sean is finished putting Hayden to bed, I'm on to my second glass of wine. It's interesting that I usually drink this stuff like it's juice, but now I'm relaxed enough to just take it easy and enjoy the explosion of flavours as I churn it in my mouth. Minutes later, when the glass is completely drained, Sean appears in the doorway.

'Need another drink?' he asks in a near whisper.

'Sounds good to me. It's not like I have to be up for work.'

Sean smiles, takes my glass, and refills it next to his. When he brings them over, he falls onto the deep cushion next to me, almost spilling the wine. I laugh aloud, and he laughs with me. For once in a long time, we're being ourselves again.

'Sorry I've been so miserable,' I tell him, resting a hand on his.

'There's nothing to be sorry for. It's been a really crazy time for you, and I couldn't imagine how hard it's been. For you *or* for Hayden.'

'Speaking of which, you two seem to be getting on.'

'Yeah, I let him in on a secret earlier.'

'Ooh, care to share?'

'I just told him about my parents, hoping it might help us connect.'

'It seems to have helped.'

Sean smiles, and we enjoy more wine together in silence. When I finish my third glass, I place it on the coffee table in front of us and lie back. My legs dangle over the arm of the sofa, my head resting in his lap. He strokes my hair ever so gently.

'Is this okay for you?' he asks.

'The stroking?'

'No, the cottage. Is it far enough away from all the Christmas stuff?'

'Oh. Yes, it's great. The problem is we can't do this every year.'

There's a small, discreet sigh coming from Sean. He tries to hide it, but I feel it in his breath and see it in his chest. Moreover, he knows I saw it. 'It's nothing,' he says. 'I just wonder what the plan is. Are we *never* going to celebrate it?'

'I'd like to. I know your siblings are big on it, so it must be a big deal for you to drop all of that just for me. But it's like I have guilt pulling me in two different directions; if I try having a normal Christmas, then it'd feel like I'm doing Nick a disservice, but if I keep hiding away from it, then I'm only ruining it for you. I just want you to know that I'm trying to find a spot in the middle. I truly don't mean to be selfish.'

'Kate, your husband was murdered on the biggest event of the year. It's perfectly normal for you to form a negative association with it. Do I want to take part in the holidays moving forward? Of course I do, but I'm willing to wait it out as long as I have to.'

'I promise I'll keep working on it.'

'Thank you.'

We smile at each other, and then he leans down and kisses me on the forehead. Sean quickly downs the remainder of his wine, then opens a conversation about the early days of our relationship. I was obviously hesitant to move on, but he was so patient with me that it sort of proved how good a man he was. Given he was a decent person and looked the way he did – still does, actually – it seemed silly not to at least give him a shot.

Some fonder memories popped up, too. Hayden's first birthday that we shared together, for instance, and how we hosted a picnic in Hyde Park, only for a stray dog to come bounding into the cake and destroying every ounce of food. That was an expensive day because Hayden was only six and quickly turned to tears. We had to take him to the LEGO shop and give him a pick of any set he wanted. Of course, he chose one that cost a couple of hundred pounds.

This was on top of his other gifts.

The stories turn to laughter. The laughter turns to romance. Before we know it, we're making love on the living room floor, enjoying each other's bodies for the first time in months while trying to keep the noise down. It feels like I've found the only man I could ever be happy with, and in this exact moment, not a single thing could bring me down.

It's cold when I wake up on the living room floor. A harsh chill creeps into the room, which strikes me as strange because the cottage has been warm all evening. Hot, even, especially after our passionate night. My eyes slowly flutter open, but it's a struggle to see in the dark. I wouldn't have woken at all if it weren't for the violent shivers my body is inflicting.

'Are you awake?' I whisper to Sean.

His snoring is all the answer I need. The throw he pulled from the sofa barely covers him as he chose to use it on me in his semi-conscious state. I fold it over and cover his shirtless body with it, kiss him on the cheek soft enough so as not to wake him, then reach for my jumper on the floor. The fabric is stone cold, but I grin and bear it while I find my feet.

I need a glass of water, so I head for the open kitchen and find my wine glass in the dark. I can't go rummaging through cupboards, so I swill out the traces of wine and replace it with cloudy tap water. I don't care because I'm so thirsty that my lips are starting to crack.

Or is that the cold?

I down the water and go to check on Hayden, but I don't make it that far. In the small passing between the living room and the kitchen, I feel an icy draft snaking through. It makes me stop, both curious and frightened at the same time as I see the front door is ajar. Carefully making my approach, I find there's no damage to the door itself, but my mind is racing in my foggy haze. Sean or I must not have locked it properly, I try to rationalise, and the wind must have blown it open. No wonder it's so damn cold.

Closing the door, I try to shake off my paranoia, silencing the voices in my head that tell me my husband's killer is still on the loose. There's no way he followed us out here, and it's silly to even suggest it. My mind is simply finding an excuse for me to keep running, but I refuse. Everything is as good as it ever can be, and that's that.

Before I return to Sean, there are two things I must do.

First, I stop by Hayden's room to check on him.

It's dark, but I can just make out the outline of him lying on his back, the duvet tucked around one leg like he always used to sleep. I can hear him snoring in a light, raspy little crackle. It's sweet, but I'm horrified to think about how fast he's growing. He's eight now, but I'll blink and he'll be twelve, fifteen, then flying the nest. We must make use of these years while we can.

Next, I close the door and head for the bedroom to grab the spare duvet. I'm feeling around in the dark, and when I get a good handful, I pull it off the bed and start making my way back to Sean. Only I don't get that far because I hear the patter of crisp paper hitting the hardwood floor. It could be anything, and I'm curious.

Turning the light on and blinding myself, I'm fully awake. The paper is by my feet in a small, folded sheet. I bend down to pick it up, dropping the duvet so I can unfold it. The words appear piece by piece, my curiosity turning to concern, then quickly to terror.

The note is for me, and it wasn't left by anyone in this cottage. Someone has been here while we were sleeping, and the sheer horror of that realisation makes me freeze in place. It wasn't paranoia after all – the killer is here somewhere. Just like I always thought, he would follow me to the ends of the earth to see that I die next. The note is proof of that, which I read and reread while holding it in weak, trembling hands:

Thought you could run from me? Think again.
I'll be seeing you real soon.

Chapter 9

Then

My honeymoon with Nick was one of the best holidays I'd ever had. We stayed at the Turtle Bay Resort in a beautiful newly-wed suite. There was a gigantic bed that we could spend all our free time in, simply loving every inch of each other. The view was something else, gazing right out across the sparkling ocean as the sun kissed the waves. The breeze was wholesome and cool, and for two weeks, I felt as though life couldn't possibly get any better.

We even got to see Pearl Harbour, as it was only an hour-long journey. There was no sense in renting a car just for the drive, so we took a tour down there. Nick filled me in on whatever the tour guide missed because he'd always loved history and had studied these kinds of things at great length. My own knowl-

edge of the event came purely from the Ben Affleck film, which, I hear, was a load of nonsense.

When the time came to leave, I felt completely refreshed. Nick and I couldn't have loved each other more than we did as we waited at the airport. It was the best time of our lives, but we missed our son so badly. It was an eighteen-hour flight that didn't even take off for another couple of hours. Even then, we had to get home, settle in, then collect Hayden from my mum.

'Want to have a final honeymoon drink?' Nick asked.

'Does a bear poop in the woods?'

We rushed to a restaurant and ordered a salad with a bottle of white wine, eating in silence as the alcohol sat well in our stomachs. There wasn't a single bad thing happening that day, save for Nick's sunburn – I had to laugh at the fact I'd tanned so nicely, but his relatively pale skin had turned lobster red. At least he didn't make a big deal out of it. He always was able to make light of a situation, even if he was the subject of the humour.

Halfway through lunch, his phone rang. He ignored it at first, but when it rang again, he excused himself and took the call. I didn't mind because we were finished eating, and I was just taking a moment to relax. I sipped more wine and reflected on what an incredible time we'd had. Nothing could have possibly disturbed me on cloud nine.

Or so I thought.

Nick returned with the bad news, except it wasn't bad as far as he was concerned. To him, it was a perfectly natural thing that had no negative repercussions whatsoever.

Personally, I was petrified.

'Your mum is having a hard time keeping Hayden contained,' he said, shoving the phone back in his pocket. 'Excited three-year-old, you know? Anyway, she gave him some chocolate to keep him happy, then he got all hyper, and now he's down for a nap.'

I thought that was the worst of it, so I just shook my head and sighed. I'd told my mother countless times not to give sugar to our son, but she never listened – apparently, it was an easy way to make him like her. Well, duh.

'Anyway,' Nick continued, 'she's messed up his nap schedule, and now she's worried about driving to meet us from the airport. She said that if she's operating a vehicle and he starts screaming again, she's scared it will make it dangerous to keep going.'

'Jesus. Why didn't she tell me this?' I asked.

'Apparently, she's been trying to call you.'

I checked my phone and saw the missed calls, along with a text saying she wouldn't be able to pick us up from Heathrow Airport. A slight panic stirred in me, but I knew Nick would solve this soon enough. 'How on earth are we going to get home?'

'There's plenty of time to figure it out,' he said calmly as ever. 'It's a long flight with an LA stop, so we'll just arrange a taxi. It's no big deal.'

I nodded loosely, grateful to have married such a rational man. Then I sat back and tried to relax. But my spine barely touched the chair before Nick snapped his fingers and reached for his phone while leaping out of his seat.

'I'll just give Ryan a call. I'm sure he'll be happy to help.'

'Yeah, I bet,' I mumbled.

Thankfully, Nick didn't hear it.

ALTHOUGH I WAS JET-LAGGED, *exhausted, and felt like fifteen cotton wool balls had been shoved into my mouth, I arrived at Heathrow Airport feeling like this was a totally fresh start. Maybe it was the sun that did it, but it suddenly seemed like my biggest concerns were no longer real.*

Ryan, in particular, was no longer a threat.

But that didn't mean I had to like him.

He met us at the arrival lounge and hugged Nick like they hadn't seen each other in years. I knew it was coming and put on my best fake smile as he then turned his attention to me and hugged me a little too tight. And, yes, his pelvis tilted my way.

As soon as his back was turned, I let out a frown and reminded myself that some people never changed. Ryan still held onto our little secret, but for as long as he was helping with the bags and hadn't yet cornered me since our return, maybe there wasn't much to worry about.

We made our way to his Galaxy. Nick took the front seat so they could catch up on the tales we'd formed in Hawaii, leaving me in the back with all the luggage. Anyone else might have felt ignored and shut out, but I was so ready to sleep that I didn't care. Besides, the less I made Ryan feel like I enjoyed his company, the better.

I didn't want to lead him on.

'So, what have my favourite couple been up to?' he asked as he navigated the roads towards London City Centre. 'Consummating the marriage, I hope.'

'Don't be crude,' Nick said. 'We had a great time. Really needed it, especially after all the drama *at the wedding. Did anyone hear back about the cause of the fire?'*

'No, but people are still calling in to ask.'

'I'm sure they'll figure it out, but I was only curious. It all worked out for the better anyway. We had the most amazing day. Thanks for helping us arrange some of it.'

'You know how much I love to take trouble off your hands.'

Ryan's eyes found me in the rear-view mirror. I wasn't sure if he'd meant I was trouble, but I started to think it could easily have been a soft hint that he was planning to take me away. God, I hoped he wasn't deluded into thinking that, but I was also aware that – as long as he was able to talk – I was one hundred per cent at his mercy.

'Are you okay?' Nick asked.

I was so deep in thought that I hadn't even realised he'd turned around in his seat. He was looking at me now, and even though his eyes had dark bags under them, they still shone that beautiful bright blue, like sun-kissed sapphire.

'Yes,' I said. 'Just looking forward to seeing Hayden.'

'Not too long now. We'll just drop the bags off and go get him.'

'I can drive you if you like,' Ryan added.

'You've done enough,' Nick said.

'I didn't get you a wedding gift, and it's been driving me mad, so at least let me do this.'

Nick agreed and thanked him. When we arrived back home, he told me he'd handle the luggage, and all I had to do was sit tight. The moment that door closed and I was completely alone with Ryan, tension filled the air as if to consume me entirely.

As soon as he spoke, the old Ryan was back.

'So you had a good time with the good doctor?' Ryan asked with a nasty snarl.

I shifted uncomfortably in my seat, unsure of how exactly to handle this. Had he developed a resentment towards Nick after all this time? A quick, uneasy glance at his eyes in the mirror told me all I needed to know – that he hated anything that stood in the way of his shot with me. If only he knew we were simply incompatible.

Now was my chance to tell him.

'Look,' I said. 'This is all getting a bit out of hand. That kiss we shared was a big mistake, and I really am sorry it happened. But Nick is your best friend, and I still see you as a good mate. We don't need to make something out of this, you know? It's unfortunate that you still have... I don't know, some kind of desire for me in one way or the other, but this has to stop. Please, just leave it alone.'

Silence filled the car.

The chilling, unsettling kind.

Ryan turned around, rocking the car under his weight. Once more, the Ryan we all knew and loved was gone, his sinister eyes finding purchase on my own soul. 'Remember when I said you and I would become an item? I wasn't joking. The very least I deserve is a passionate night with you, after all you put me through.'

'What did I put you through?'

'Seriously? You led me on, dated me even though you wanted my best mate.'

'What? No, that's wrong. I didn't even know Nick at the time—'

'Shut it!'

My head snapped back, barely able to believe the aggressive nature of his tone. I looked around outside the car, hoping Nick would be back any second. As if God himself were answering my prayers, the car boot opened with a rubbery hiss. Nick leaned in, grabbed the last bag and suitcase, then shot me a wink.

'Last trip. Won't be long.'

When the door shut, I thought about getting out

and joining him. But there was a massive flaw in that plan: Ryan was more than capable of telling him about the kiss. There still a chance Nick would forgive me if I just took the time to explain, but why risk such a thing after the perfect wedding and honeymoon? This was supposed to be a fresh start.

And my bad decisions were already ruining it.

'So, what's it going to be?' Ryan asked.

'What?'

'Are we going to screw, or does hubby need to know we kissed?'

'You can't seriously expect me to sleep with you?'

'Damn right I can. And you're on a time limit.'

It occurred to me then that my whole marriage was in Ryan's hands. He was a nutcase, completely and utterly undone by his bitter jealousy of Nick. It was evident he would cross mountains to get what he wanted – face armies, maybe even burn fortresses to the ground.

Or wedding venues.

The puzzle pieces fell into place. My mind had rejected the theory this whole time, simply because I didn't want to believe he could do such a thing. But knowing the source of the fire was still undiscov-

ered, coupled with the fact we hadn't seen Ryan for a couple of hours that night, it was impossible not to at least consider him the suspect.

'Did you start the fire?' I asked.

'What?' His mouth hung open in disbelief.

'Don't play dumb. Did you or did you not start the fire at our wedding?'

'Are you joking?'

'Yes or no?'

'Kate, I love you, and I want you. I'll never stop until I have you, but I'm not an arsonist. A blackmailer, maybe, but not an arsonist.' He huffed, shot me a disgusted glare, and then turned in his seat to face the road. 'Think about my offer. Tick-tock.'

I opened my mouth to tell him he was a creep and that I would never spend the night with him, but I stopped when I realised I might not have much of a choice. Ryan had me by the proverbial balls on this one, and there was nothing I could think of other than to call his bluff.

By the time I was ready to say it aloud, the car door opened. Nick sunk into the seat.

'All right, gang, let's get out of here,' he said.

I wished I could.

Chapter 10
Now

My breath is juddery as I try to make sense of what I read. My husband's killer, right here in the middle of Deepwood Forest? It's not possible, or at least it shouldn't be. It must be some kind of sick joke, but who would do such a thing?

More importantly, are we safe?

The very first thing I do is shove the note into my pyjama pocket and dart into the next room. I suddenly no longer care about the coldness in the cottage because I'm sweating from head to toe at the fact that somebody was here – somebody had actually entered the building while we were sleeping and left that paper on the bed.

Hayden's bedroom door smashes open and hits the wall. I flick the light switch and flood the room with bright light, then check the room over as fast as possible. Hayden sits up slowly, rubbing his eyes and groaning at the very sight of me.

'What's going on?' he asks.

'Someone is in the cottage. Get out of bed and come with me.'

As soon as I confirm the room is clear, I take Hayden by the hand and march him into the living room. Once more, I turn on a light and deal with annoyed muttering from Sean. He barely moves until I pull the throw off him and put the note in his hand.

'What's this?' he grumbles.

'Someone has been here while we slept.'

'Oh, you had a bad dream.'

'No, the *killer* was here.'

'Are you sure you're not being paranoid?'

'Read the note!'

Sean's eyes widen at the sound of my voice. He finally sits up, unfolding the note as I had only a minute or so ago. I hold Hayden close to me, watching Sean as his eyes move back and forth across the page, reading it over and over like his brain just can't comprehend.

'Is this some kind of joke?' he asks.

'Absolutely not.'

'Then how did...? I mean, when did...?'

'Will you please get up and do something?'

'Like what?'

'Mum.' Hayden tugs my hand. 'Is someone in the cottage?'

I don't know what to tell him, and I don't know what to do. All I can manage is a sharp look at Sean, who seems to finally be waking up as he hurries into his jeans and shoes, then starts to check every square inch of the cottage. Meanwhile, I grab the fire poker from its sheath and wrap my arms around my son, clutching them tight in case someone comes at us.

In case *he* comes at us.

Sean returns a couple of minutes later, shrugging and then scratching his head as he gives the note one last read. He doesn't look any less confused as he looks up at me, holding it up for me to see. 'Where did you find this?'

'On our bed. And the front door was open.'

'Unlocked or open?'

'Wide open,' I say, trying not to sound short with him.

'Well, there's nobody here now. I bet this is someone just playing with us.'

I can hardly believe what he's saying. Sean is

usually the only man in the world who I can rely on for absolutely everything, but this doesn't seem to be scaring him like it is me and Hayden. In fact, he doesn't seem like he even believes it's real.

'Why aren't you reacting?' I ask.

'It's nothing.' He pauses. 'It's just that the odds of him coming all this way are quite slim. Where is he hiding? In the forest? With the neighbours?'

I know he's just trying to be realistic, but that does give me an idea. I shrug, realise I'm still holding the poker, then let go of it and Hayden at the same time. Thankfully, he knows better than to walk away from me after all that's happened.

'Maybe it was them,' I say gently.

'The neighbours?' he asks with disbelief. 'Frank and Jeanie?'

'Who else could it possibly be?'

'And you suppose... what? That they somehow know all about you, wrote the note to mess with your head, then crept in here while we were sleeping and left this message? I don't mean to sound dismissive, but they have no motive whatsoever. Especially if it's just a prank.'

I hate to admit it, but he's right. Sometimes you just get a sense of people, and the sense I got from Frank and Jeanie was that they're basically good people. Even by the very slight chance that they know about Nick's murder, why would they think this was a good idea?

'I think we need to sleep,' Sean says.

'Sleep? But how?'

'You sleep in Hayden's room with him. You're both all right with that?'

Hayden and I nod at the same time.

'What will you do?' I ask.

'I'm going to hold that poker and watch the room all night. If anyone dares to come in again, they'll very much regret it.' Sean reaches for the poker and drags out a chair, then hesitates. 'There is one other thing.'

'What's that?'

He pauses, looking troubled. 'Let me talk with you alone for a moment.'

I DOUBLE-CHECK Hayden's room is secure and that the window is locked, then put him to bed. He's at the age now where he likes to pretend nothing bothers him because it's cool to be that way, but I'm his mother. Which means I easily see his leg twitching every two seconds.

After assuring him he's safe and explaining I'll

be there in a minute to sleep on the floor beside the bed, he rolls over and pulls the duvet up to his chin, kicking one leg out as usual. I then dim the lights and return to Sean.

'What did you want to talk about?' I ask, still feeling a little rattled myself.

Sean is sitting on a small wooden chair that he's dragged to the entrance of the narrow hallway. It rocks back under his weight as he pats the fire poker. He reminds me of an old deputy, guarding the locked-up cowboy until the sheriff returns from his duties.

It makes me feel safe.

'In light of what's happened,' he says, 'do you think we should still stay here?'

'The thought did cross my mind.'

'And?'

'We can't go back. Malcolm isn't coming to pick us up for a few more days.'

'I could walk back through the forest and get him to drive back up?'

'Leaving us alone up here with that psycho?'

It's obvious from the way he starts to roll his eyes that he doesn't believe the note is real. However, I do appreciate that he's making an effort not to show it. 'Okay then, what about you making the walk?'

'I don't know. Malcolm kept saying how dangerous it is. And you saw the terrain.'

'That doesn't leave us with a whole lot of options, does it?'

'There's always Frank and Jeanie.'

'What about them?'

'Maybe they have a car.'

'I didn't see one. Anyway, for all we know, they're the ones who wrote the note.'

Instead of arguing that out, I simply nod and try to stay focused. I highly doubt the neighbours had anything to do with that. Even if they know about Nick's murder, they would have to be incredibly nimble to sneak past us in the dark.

Nimble like *he* is.

The stress is easily readable in Sean's face. He's trying his best to protect us, but we're stuck in the middle of nowhere, and the only hope of returning to civilisation for help means leaving his family up here alone. Well, not exactly alone.

The killer is up here.

'We're out of options,' Sean says defeatedly.

'What about in the morning?' I offer.

'You mean to walk through the forest?'

'Yes.'

'I have a feeling it's not going to be any better. It's funny, as we were coming up here in the jeep, I was watching the ground and wondering if we might have made it by foot. Without suitcases and you two at my side, there's a small chance I could traverse it. It would take a whole lot of slow, careful foot placement, but it's possible.'

All I can do is shake my head. 'We're coming full circle here. If you go, we're alone and exposed. Unless we stay with Frank and Jeanie, but you don't want to trust anyone.' I sigh and move to the window, staring out at the small mess of trees glowing under the moonlight. Beyond that is pitch-black. The whole forest has swallowed us.

We're in the belly of the beast.

'Let's stick to plan A,' Sean says, coming up behind me. I hear him put down the fire poker, and then both his arms come around to hold me steady. He can probably feel me shaking. 'I'll keep an eye on you both. Trust me. We brought enough food supplies with us, so maybe we can just stick it out and still find a way to enjoy the trip, and we brought enough food with us to last the entire time.'

'Even though someone is out there?'

'It's either that or stay locked up in a room for a few days.'

'So we're screwed either way?'

'Pretty much.'

Although I try to steady my breathing, a long, ragged sigh escapes me. I'm not trying to be difficult, but while the killer is out there, it's hard to relax. That doesn't mean we can't try though – as long as Sean is looking out for us, we should be fine.

'Will you do something else for me?' I ask, feeling him nuzzle into my neck.

'Anything.'

'Could you check the perimeter one more time before bed?'

'No problem at all.'

Sean grabs the fire poker, rests it on his shoulder, and slips his boots on. 'Lock the door behind me. Don't open it unless I knock six times. No more, no less. But don't worry, I have a feeling everything is going to be just fine.'

I smile half-heartedly and follow his instructions, locking me and my son up in the cottage alone. I really appreciate how hard my boyfriend is trying to make us feel like we can sleep through the night and not get butchered, but the words on the note are still buzzing around in my head, like an angry wasp that just won't leave me alone.

I'll be seeing you real soon.

I'll be seeing you real soon.

I'll be seeing you real soon.

SEAN RETURNED JUST five minutes later, then sent me off to bed. Hayden was asleep when I joined him, so I put a pillow on the floor and laid my head down. I can watch the window from where I lie, the moonlight casting silhouettes of the forest. Movement catches my eye every five seconds, refusing to let me sleep. I know Sean is protecting us in the hallway, but that doesn't stop the cold touch of fear from grasping my spine. I'm finding it hard to breathe, and every time I close my eyes, all I see is the blood pooling around Nick's lifeless body. It was the worst moment of my life, and somehow, it's still messing with me.

I thought hiding away in the forest was a good thing. That bloody Christmas wasn't supposed to surface in my conscience at all, but here I am thinking of every awful second from the day that changed my life; Nick telling me he'll be right back, *Home Alone 2* playing in the background, and me discovering the body a few minutes later. I'll never forget that horrible sight, standing in the kitchen and knowing our lives were instantly wrecked while Macaulay Culkin merrily set up an inflatable man in his hotel suite. It struck me then as it strikes me now – that Christmas is a happy time for many, but for us, it will never be the same.

That's why I try to avoid it at all costs. I just didn't think it would follow me here. The killer wants me, too, after I saw him fleeing the scene. A simple police report was all it took, and now he's back to finish me off. Maybe even Hayden, too.

But no matter how hard I try to convince myself we'll be okay, the same question keeps popping up in my mind, like one of those annoying windows on a computer that are determined to sell you things you don't need. I wish I could click this thought away, but it's ingrained in me now. It's a part of me.

How? it asks.

How is he here?

Chapter 11
Then

I HADN'T HEARD *from Ryan in weeks, and life was finally getting good again. Nick and I were better than ever, loving each other just as much as we had during our first year as a couple. Hayden was growing before my very eyes, even in that short space of time. Nick had made some extravagant purchases, and none of them seemed to hit us too hard. There wasn't a single thing worth complaining about, and better yet, Ryan was gone.*

I felt kind of sorry for him in a way. It was never my intention to lead him on or to make him think something could happen between us. That night we kissed was just a dumb, exhausted mistake that should never have occurred. Ryan's absence since picking us up suggested that perhaps he'd come around and was starting to realise that. At least I hoped so.

Because he was starting to scare me.

Christmas was right around the corner, and we were all extremely excited. Nick and I were putting up the decorations, him hanging the chain links from each corner of the ceiling while Hayden and I decorated the tree. As was tradition, Michael Bublé filled the room with that perfect voice of his. Nick tried to sing over it, of course, making Hayden scream at him to stop. I couldn't help but laugh, trying to distract him with a musical reindeer decoration that he could hang on one of the branches. It did the job, making Hayden poke out his tongue as he reached high above his head to hang the loop around the branch.

Something I never expected to happen – especially on a day like that – did, in fact, occur. There was a knock on our door. Living in the penthouse, most of the mail just went into a slot downstairs or got left in the lobby. The elevator coming up to our floor was reserved for personal visitors, and we weren't expecting anyone.

When Nick and I were finished staring at each other with confused, scrunched-up faces, he climbed down from the stepladder and went for the door. I continued decorating with Hayden. It wasn't until I heard his voice that my blood ran cold.

'Nicky boy!' Ryan yelled from the front door.

'This is kind of a bad time,' Nick told him.

'It won't take long. I just wondered if I could borrow Kate for a while.'

'We're decorating the flat right now.'

'Please. It's about your Christmas present.'

While Nick went quiet to contemplate this, my nerves were fried. The last thing I wanted was to have to spend time with Ryan, and something told me this wasn't just about a present. I waited, nothing else existing in that long, drawn-out time, until Nick finally replied.

'Kate!' he called. 'Would you mind joining Ryan for a while?'

I blew out a fed-up breath and scooped Hayden into my arms. He protested a little while I went to the door, once more wearing the most sincere-looking smile I could muster. Both the guys turned to look at me, and since Nick had his back turned, Ryan's evil eyes looked me up and down like a monster drooling over his meal.

'What's up?' I asked.

'I want to buy Nick something cool,' he said. 'I wondered if you might come and take a look for me.

I already know where to find it, so maybe it will take an hour or less. If you don't mind, it would be so helpful.'

'This really isn't a good time.'

'But it's for my present,' Nick said.

'What about the decorations?'

'They can wait.'

'But Hayden—'

'I'll take care of Hayden.'

In a heartbeat, Nick took our son from my arms and left me with no more excuses. I stood there like an idiot, doing my best to think of a good reason why I couldn't spend time alone with Ryan. All the while, he was sneering at me because he knew he had me cornered.

As usual, he was getting exactly what he wanted.

And I wouldn't dare say no to him.

WE WALKED *in silence to Marylebone Green, a spacious park with not much to look at. This place was absolutely beautiful in the summer – like it'd been picked out of a fantasy novel or something – but right now, it was just naked trees and grass that'd given up under the harsh cold. I never did* like parks in the winter, and the temperature had dropped drastically since Hayden's recent birthday picnic. Instead of offering sun and warm days, now the open expanses were simply dishing out colds.

Still, nothing made me feel more of a chill than Ryan.

He took a seat overlooking a large pond, but he didn't bother looking me in the eye.

'Sit,' he said.

Even if I wanted to, benches in the winter were too uncomfortable for my liking. 'I'm happy standing,' I told him. 'Look, I'm guessing there is no present for Nick? That it was just a lame excuse to get me out here alone?'

'You don't think much of me, do you?'

'Not in recent weeks, no.'

Ryan nodded as if he finally understood how much of a creep he'd been. But the way his face changed like the wind, I wondered if he was even capable of linear thought. I could only imagine how chaotic it was in his sick little brain.

'I took some time out,' he said, 'to try and gain a little perspective on this.'

'Uh-huh. What were your findings?'

'Basically, that you're a slut.'

It took everything I had not to slap him again.

Instead, I opted for a deep sigh and sat down next to him, much to my chagrin. I watched the pond with him, realising how still it looked. Almost as if it were dead. I matched my voice to the calmness.

'I told you before, what happened was never supposed to happen. I was exhausted and did something dumb. You're not going to hold it against me forever. I won't let you.'

Ryan raised an eyebrow and met my gaze. 'You're acting like you're in control.'

'Well, I am. This is my life. My marriage. My body. You don't get to dictate what happens.' As I spoke each word and punctuated his perverse absurdity, I felt the heat rising in my chest until it burned out of my throat like dragon flame. I hadn't intended to sound nasty, but it was about time I took a stand. It came out however it was destined to. 'And one more thing: stop sending me pictures of your junk. It's not worth bragging about.'

'Oh, you little...'

The Mr. Nice Guy routine was gone. Ryan ground his teeth and shook his head like he was doing all he could not to lash out at me physically. I found myself looking around to make sure we weren't alone. Thankfully, there were plenty of dog walkers nearby. I stood to make sure they could see me, but Ryan stood, too, stepping towards me and urging me back until my heel hit the small dividing gate that barricaded the pond.

'What I was going to say, if you let me finish,' he spat angrily, with ire burning in his eyes like hot coals, 'is that I've decided to give you some time. I appreciate that you'll have to cheat on your perfect husband, and that can't be easy. So you have until Christmas Day to come to my flat and spread your legs like the slut you are. Otherwise, your secret gets out.'

I was stunned, fear sucking the energy from my legs. I wanted to fall and cry, but I had to be strong. Or at least appear that way when confronted by the enemy.

'You know what? Just do it. Tell Nick.'

It was a bluff, and he knew it. So did the chilling winds that shared our filthy little secret. We exchanged a long, hard stare, but I knew I was losing. Ryan had lost all sense of reason and shame, and now I realised for certain there was no way out of it without meeting his demands and spending the night with him.

Or to let Nick find out about our meaningless kiss.

'Christmas Day,' he said. 'One way or the other.'

Ryan turned on his heel and left me standing there by the pond. Was it normal to feel this much shame after a kiss? It wasn't like I'd slept with the guy – not yet anyway, but the pressure was pushing me that way. The real betrayal was that it was Nick's best friend. The best man at his wedding and all-time favourite buddy. It made me feel sick with guilt that I'd stooped so low, and now I was paying for it by way of malicious blackmail.

Maybe this was what I deserved.

CHRISTMAS WAS COMING AROUND FAST. There was only a week to go, and I was absolutely terrified of what might happen. Just to be clear, I wasn't a slut. There wasn't a single part of me that wanted to spend the night with Ryan. Even given the circumstances, I really didn't see myself in a room alone with him, much less a bed. Which really only left one option.

One night, on a Friday when our wonderful little family had fish and chips while gathered around the TV to watch Moana struggle with her journey, I found my appetite had vanished. I looked around at everyone – at Nick, who was reclined on the two-seater. At Hayden, who was lying on his back between Nick's legs, staring intently with a slight smile as his hand hovered in front of his mouth with a piece of fruit. They were in the moment, enjoying the family time without a single other care in the world because they loved and felt loved in return.

I couldn't have felt worse.

My phone buzzed. I had a quick check and saw another text from Ryan. It was just a short one to tell me this was my last chance. I felt so stressed. Everything around me was about to come crumbling down under the weight of that one bloody mistake. How horrible a person was I to keep this to myself for so long?

'Everything okay?' Nick asked.

'It's fine,' I told him, putting down my phone and smiling.

'You sure? You've gone a bit pale.'

'Yeah, a friend from school has been in a car accident.'

That part was actually true, though I'd received the text from my friend's mother earlier in the day. Even if he checked my phone now, he'd still see that message. As long as he didn't look at the time stamp. It occurred to me then that I was plotting – thinking up new lies on the spot to cover up my old ones. I couldn't have felt worse.

Nick tried to console me, but I told him my friend and I had distanced over the years and that I was feeling okay. He didn't seem convinced, but we managed to watch the rest of the film in peace. By the end, Hayden had fallen asleep on his dad with his mouth open and his head rolled back. We handled it as a team – me scooping up his head and pushing down the recliner, while Nick then picked Hayden up and carried him into bed. When he was safely tucked in, we stood in the doorway watching him for a moment, grinning like idiots as our son's chest rose and fell, his stuffed little airways making him snore like a sleeping puppy.

'We made that,' Nick said.

'We did,' I said with a smile.

'Maybe we should talk about making another.'

My head spun so fast that the world turned to a blur for a second. I gazed deep into Nick's eyes and immediately knew I was ready. I nodded, telling him it was a good idea, but in the back of my mind was still the problem with Ryan. What exactly was I supposed to do? Put my life on hold while that creep continued to threaten me?

I needed advice, and I needed it badly. After

telling Nick I was too tired to make love to him that night, he fell asleep, and I turned my phone back on. I drafted a text to my mother, telling her we needed to talk as soon as possible. She wasn't who I'd normally turn to, but I couldn't risk other people knowing how bad I'd been.

How close I was to tearing my family apart.

Chapter 12

Now

THE NIGHT WAS rough and sleepless, but the morning is no better. Sean has prepared a cooked breakfast for the family, which helps but doesn't fix the whole situation. We all eat in silence, most likely all thinking the same thing: can't we leave?

I keep running it through my mind as if there must be some way of making it happen. But there's not. Sean could head through the forest for help, but even if – and I mean *if* – he makes it down to Malcolm's house in one piece, Hayden and I could be murdered while we wait. The phones are dead – a consequence of staying in the middle of nowhere, I suppose.

It doesn't leave a whole lot of options but to stick it out.

'We might as well make the most of it while we're here,' Sean says while Hayden runs to the bathroom. 'We've got five more days of this, so there's no point locking ourselves away in a cottage the whole time.'

'What do you suggest? And if you say camping, I swear to God—'

'Nothing that extreme.' Sean smiles, but it's forced. 'Look, Hayden is a young lad. Like all young lads, he wants to run and climb and burn off some energy. Now, I know he isn't the most energetic kid in the world, but maybe we could go for a walk with him. Get some air, change the scenery, and so on.'

'What about the killer?'

'It's one against three in broad daylight. Even if he comes running at us with a knife, I'm pretty sure we could put him on the ground before...' He hesitates, probably noticing the sadness in my eyes. 'Sorry, that's so insensitive.'

'It's okay.'

'But you get my point?'

Although it's a tough call to make, he's probably right. When Hayden gets back, I ask if it's something he'd be interested in, and his eyes light up for the first time today. I guess that settles it, so we shower – taking it in turns watching the door, of course – then get our warmer clothes on and head into the forest for a walk.

Sean tells me he spotted a trail when he went looking for Hayden, so we relocate it and enjoy a slow, steady walk. Hayden is running off into the distance, but he keeps coming back when we remind him not to leave our sight. It's interesting – I can feel the tension leave my body, my problems falling to the back of my mind. Every now and then, I look behind us just to make sure we're not being followed, but overall, I'm glad we did this.

'Thank you,' I tell Sean.

'For what?'

'Everything. For sacrificing time with your sisters on Christmas, for watching the door all night, and for talking me into coming out here today.' I take a deep breath, smelling wet bark and pine. It's like a car air freshener, only less invasive on the senses. It's as if I'm a new person, no matter how temporary it might be.

We continue through the trail for around twenty minutes. There are stones in my boots, but I grew used to it a little while ago. I'm enjoying this too much for a little discomfort to bother me, and it only pops into my head now that Christmas could be any day now. It could be tomorrow, for all I know. I've lost all sense of time due to worry.

Sean takes my hand. He must have read my mind, or at least my facial expression. I grin at him while Hayden passes us with an adventurous roar, swinging a long stick around like it's some kind of sword. I couldn't be happier, and not a thing could go wrong.

Until I hear the snap.

It came from behind us. I stop dead in my tracks and spin around. Sean is asking me what's wrong, but I shush him and Hayden both, hoping to listen harder. It must sound again, I tell myself. If it doesn't, then it's all in my head, and I can pass it off as paranoia. I wait for what seems forever. Then, when I'm ready to carry on walking, it happens again.

'There,' I say in a harsh, cracking voice. 'You hear that?'

'Definitely,' Sean whispers.

Hayden has come up behind me and is tugging on my coat for comfort. I put an arm around him as I stare into the trees, expecting my husband's killer to come dashing out at us any minute now. My body has gone numb, all sorts of crazy thoughts hurtling through my mind. Are we safe now, or has he come to finish what he started?

'I'll check it out,' Sean says.

But who knows if he'll come back?

'Maybe we should just return to the cottage,' I say under my breath because if there is someone in the trees, it's likely they can hear every word we say. I don't want them knowing our plan.

But Sean is already taking the stick from Hayden and checking its weight. It seems he approves because he gives a little nod and then kisses me on the cheek. 'It's going to be okay,' he tells me so convincingly I almost believe him. 'But if I shout run, you run. Don't wait for me, and don't look back – just head for the cottage and lock the doors. Understood?'

I tell him I understand, but the way he's talking sounds so terrifyingly final. It's like he's not planning on coming back at all, as if this will be his final defence for our family and we'll never see him again. I find myself praying silently.

I don't want to lose another one.

I just can't.

Sean takes his first step towards the trees, then disappears into the brush. Hayden clings closer to me. I hold him tight because nobody will hurt him for as long as there's a single breath left in my body. That's the one thing I'm sure of.

We wait in silence, wondering if there's any real reason to be afraid. Twigs and branches snap all the time, but it doesn't mean someone is out there watching us. I glance back at the trail we'd come through and question how fast we can run. I never was very athletic – Hayden can probably run faster than I can.

But maybe that's all that matters.

'Mum, I'm scared,' he says in a ragged breath.

'It's going to be okay,' I tell him, possibly lying – I don't know yet.

There's a stirring in the trees. A single bird flees the scene, rustling the branches. It should be clear in there, with nothing but sticks and trunks, but the bushes and thicket are so dense that it only lends to the darkness. There's no natural sunlight, which means no way of seeing my boyfriend as he ventures into the danger zone on our behalf.

Then, silence.

It's too unbearably long. I can't stand it.

'Sean?' I call out, then wait impatiently for a response.

What if he's hurt? What if that bird fled because it witnessed something brutal? I would never forgive myself for letting another one die. How bad a person am I that I'm the one who survives hell while those who love me suffer? Is that why Nick died? Because I'm cursed?

Motion stirs in the trees. The bush moves. Hayden takes a giant step back, letting go and getting ready to run. I clench my fist as if I can fight, but in reality, I'm only going to run. Just like Sean told me to. My eyes don't leave the bush because if the killer steps out now, then I want to be ready for him. It moves again. My nerves are on fire. My legs trembling. My breath caught in my throat and threatening to suffocate me.

Sean steps out, shrugging and dropping the stick.

'False alarm,' he says as if we didn't just fear for our lives.

Words struggle to come. I stutter and make a weird, empty sound before I finally manage to speak. 'False alarm?' I say. 'You didn't find anything?'

'No. I searched around, but there's no sign of a human being out there at all. No footprints, no pressed brambles, nothing. I think being out here is maybe starting to get to you. Perhaps it's time we head back and put the kettle on.'

I hate to say it, but he's right. We've come far enough, pushed our luck, and even if it wasn't the killer on this occasion, there's nothing to suggest he's not still there somewhere – watching, waiting. Biding his time.

Until the opportunity comes to take our lives.

EVENING HAS COME AROUND FAST. The sun has already set, shrouding the cottage in absolute darkness. When I looked out the window earlier, the only light in the entire scene was that of the neighbour's living room. I found it too creepy to stay close to a window, so after putting Hayden to bed, I came straight here into the bathroom to assess my messy appearance.

I can hardly look at myself. My usually neat, mousy-brown hair looks frayed and worn. It's only been a couple of days, but this is what stress and sleep deprivation does to me. My eyes are bloodshot, with deep bags sagging underneath them. My skin is two shades lighter. Somehow, I've aged ten years in just a few hours.

'Everything okay in there?' Sean asks.

I tell him it's fine, but it's a lie. The truth is, I'm really starting to freak out. Not just because the killer may very well be out here in Nowhereville with us, but because I have another secret I'm yet to tell. It might soon be time to tell it, just to ease the pressure on my already suffocating soul.

After splashing a bit of water on my face and running a vented brush through my hair, I open the bathroom door and step out. I had every intention of putting on a brave face, but I crack the second I see Sean standing in the kitchen. He's staring out the window as if on high alert, which only serves as a reminder of how much trouble we might be in. I go to him, wrapping my arms around him and squeezing so tight it probably hurts.

'Whoa. What's wrong?' he asks, moving my hands only to turn around. Then he embraces me, holding me in his strong arms and truly making me feel like nothing can hurt me. 'You just need a hug? That's fine by me.'

It's more than a hug. It's everything to me. My entire world fell apart long ago, but I've been holding on for dear life. I thought we were doing okay for eleven months of the year, but I'm now learning that was wrong the whole time. The killer *does* want me, he *is* somewhere in the forest, and there's *nothing* we can do about it.

'It feels like these are our last days,' I mumble into Sean's chest.

'They are,' he says, still holding tight. 'We'll be out of here soon.'

'I mean our last few days of life.'

He comes away then, holding my shoulders and finding me with those emerald eyes. 'Nothing is going to happen to you, you hear? For as long as I'm around, you won't so much as find yourself within ten feet of the killer.'

'You promise?'

'I promise.'

Don't ask how, but I believe him. Even if it feels like the end, I know Sean will be there for us. It's the same reason I fell in love with him in the first place – his strong, confident nature was a good mix with his sensitivity and kindness. He reminded me of Nick, and he still does, though I won't tell him that. I fear it may upset him, and if it upsets him, he might leave. It's not that I'm using him, but I'm well aware that he's our safety blanket.

If he goes, Hayden and I are as good as dead.

Chapter 13
Then

IT PHYSICALLY HURT me that I had to lie to Nick, but I needed to be free the next morning. My mother had agreed to meet on the condition that we do it over coffee at ten o'clock. The thing with her was that if she said to be there at a certain time and you were late, she would get up and walk away before the minute hand moved more than once.

The lie was a short, simple one: Mum needed my advice on something and wanted to see me. It was Nick's day off from the surgery, so he took Hayden in his arms, promised him a fun day, then told me he hoped my mum was okay. That was Nick for you: kind and helpful.

It made me feel sick.

My mother was waiting for me in a surprisingly

grand café called the Ivy. It was packed out, so I thought myself lucky she'd reserved a table and thought about dining ahead of time. She'd ordered us both a toasted cheese sandwich and a pot of coffee in advance, which – considering the place was packed with conversing patrons – saved a lot of time.

I lowered myself into the chair she'd chosen in the corner, where the plush seating supported her back. As usual, she left me in one of the awkward wooden chairs that wreaked havoc on my spine. I forgave it, however, as she was there simply out of support.

'What's bothering you?' she asked, getting straight to the point as always.

I didn't hold back. Any ounce of shame I'd felt until now was instantly doubled. My mother had always held remarkably high standards for people, most of whom failed to reach those standards. It was the same for me, constantly tripping over my own feet to get approval. The situation I was in wouldn't help, but I needed the advice so badly that I no longer cared.

To her credit, she didn't say a single word while I told her the whole truth. She only broke eye contact with me when it meant reaching for her coffee. I'd talked her ear off, forgetting my own coffee and rushing for it as soon as I was finished. Partly because my lips were dry and partly because it hid my humiliated face. The coffee was bitter anyway.

Or was that just the vibe in the room?

When she was ready to talk, my mother set down her cup, cleared her throat, and leaned on her elbows, tucking her knuckles under her chin. She always did this when she had something harsh to say, so I prepared myself for a vicious attack.

'You need to tell him' was all she said.

I could hardly believe my ears. My chin could've touched the table. 'What?'

'You heard me. You've betrayed a man – a good man – and he has a right to know. It's no use jumping into bed with someone just to shut him up. I went to university, dear, so take it from me. The only way to silence this... Ricky?'

'Ryan.'

'The only way to silence Ryan is to take away his power. The only way to do that is by telling the secret he's keeping. If you're not going to do it for that reason alone, then do it out of respect for the father of your child. You love him, don't you?'

'Of course I do.'

'Then act like it. Tell him the truth.'

It's not like I hadn't thought of that, but hearing it from a different generation of woman made it crystal clear. The thing was, it wasn't going to be a comfortable conversation. Not that I deserved it anyway – I thought of myself as a monster.

'What about Hayden?' I asked.

'What about him?'

'If Nick leaves me because of this, his life will never be the same.'

My mother shook her head and tutted. 'You can hide behind your three-year-old all you like, but we both know the only reason you're hesitating is because you're scared. Now, listen to me, Kate, and listen well.' She leaned in closer, locking me in with her steely gaze. 'I raised you better than to cheat on your husband, but I never thought I'd have to convince you to do the right thing when it came to telling him. Don't be a coward. Tell him.'

There it was, as easy as that. She'd always had a way of putting things so bluntly that they hammered sense into me. It may not be nice to hear, but it was true. I'd been a bad person, a terrible wife, and maybe I had been using Hayden's security as an excuse. It was time I stood up and faced my fears, doing the right thing no matter how hard it was.

And if Nick left me? Well, it was the least I deserved.

But at least Ryan could no longer threaten me.

I PAID *for the brunch and coffee as a way of saying thank you, then headed back to the flat. I'd never been so scared in all my life as I was in that moment. Nick was about to find out the truth, and it was quite possible that my family would fall apart.*

All because of a stupid kiss.

I bolstered myself as much as possible, running a whole bunch of speeches in my head. None of them was coherent because my mind was a mess of overlaps, desperately reaching from one excuse to the other, picking out words and dropping them elsewhere to make it work. The truth was, none of it would work.

None of it, except simply coming clean.

Outside the flat's main door, I took one last, deep breath, then turned my key in the lock and let myself in. I'd been half expecting to see Nick and Hayden chilling out in front of the TV, so it came as quite a shock when Hayden was standing by the door in the suit he'd worn at the wedding. His shirt was unbuttoned at the top, and the jacket was miss-

ing, but I recognised it as a makeshift version of the same attire from our special day.

'Hayden?' I said, laughing. 'What are you doing?'

'Come with me, miss,' he said, then stomped clumsily into the dining room.

I followed, with no idea what was going on except my son had become a little maître d'.

When I entered the dining room, it suddenly became clear.

There were candles and lights everywhere. Nick was wearing a fancy but casual blue shirt that made his eyes shine. He was grinning from ear-to-ear, standing by the dining room table with a tea towel over one arm as he stood up unnaturally straight. Hayden tottered over to him, mumbled up at him, and then Nick pulled out a chair for me.

'If you would, Madame.'

His infectious smile got me, and I was grinning, too. I took the seat and watched as father and son served up a pasta dish that I really had no room for, but I would eat simply because of the effort that had gone into it. I must have been blushing.

'What's going on?' I asked curiously.

'He wanted to play Restaurants,' Nick whispered in my ear. 'I decided we might as well make *use of it and go all out. So we cooked lunch together, prepared the table, and now you're the guest of honour. Enjoy.'*

Nick then planted a kiss on my cheek, making me feel a violent swirl of emotions. My love for these two was endless, and I also felt a shiver of raw attraction as his warm breath landed on my neck. When he moved away and I caught a whiff of his cologne – Armani, one of my favourites – it was like we were on our first date again.

Only this time, we had a little man with us.

'Eat your food, Mummy,' Hayden said, tucking in.

Okay, so there were some things yet to be learned, but he would only do so by trying. I'd never seen anyone try this hard, either. What a blessing it was to have these two in my life. Could I really let out a painful secret and destroy all of this in a heartbeat?

Not really, but I had to. It just had to wait a few more hours.

No matter how anxious it made me.

LATER THAT NIGHT, *I made what you might call a guilt meal. I felt like such a horrible wife that it was almost deserved to have one last meal before what could be the end. I wasn't quite sure how this was going to pan out.*

But I did know I was stalling.

After we washed the dishes side by side, like we always did, regardless of who'd cooked, we put Hayden to bed together for the last time. Everything we did felt so final. Some might say I was being overdramatic, but with how well my husband had treated me since the day we met, I wouldn't blame him for no longer wanting to be with me.

I mean, I'd kissed his best friend, for crying out loud.

We made it all the way to bedtime, lying next to each other and wearing very little. Nick had his nose buried in a book about the root of social anxiety disorder in children. He'd read excerpts to me on a nightly basis, and it really was fascinating, but tonight, I was so distracted by what was about to happen that I'd barely heard his voice.

'Kate?' he said, putting down his book and clearly sensing something. 'What's wrong?'

'We need to talk,' I told him before I could talk myself out of it.

'Okay...'

I took a deep breath, then blurted it out. 'I kissed Ryan.'

The room went silent and still. Neither of us said a word, and I couldn't bring myself to look him in the eye. I waited for him to tell me it was over – that I'd betrayed his trust and he didn't want to be with me any longer.

Imagine my surprise when he laughed.

'What's so funny?' I asked, feeling ridiculously small now.

'I already knew about it.'

'You did?'

'Hayden told me.'

Relief flooded through me, suddenly releasing weeks of worry. I couldn't believe I'd held onto it for so long, and now that it was out there, I laughed a little, too. Though my own laughter was more like an awkward giggle.

'Yeah, he said he saw you two on the sofa. Apparently, you kissed him on the cheek, or vice versa. The poor little guy thought it was something more than that. I had to explain how adults do that to be friendly sometimes. He had a hard time getting his head around it.'

My heart sank into my stomach. I was back where I had been, harbouring a secret that was likely to tear us apart. Only now, it was harder to explain because he'd already been misled. Not only had I lied to my son about the kiss, but it'd got back to Nick anyway. Now we were all living in that lie, and all I had for company was remorse.

Nick kissed me on the head and returned to his book, still giving off a short, under-the-breath chuckle. He'd dismissed it entirely, not believing for a second that I would do something like that to him. I really was a horrible person.

At least one thing was clear. Well, two things: first, I absolutely had to set this straight. Second, there was no longer a glimmer of hope for this family's survival. I thought about how I'd tucked a happy Hayden into bed, and with Christmas coming along in just a few days, I wanted one last good Christmas with my family before it all came crashing down around me.

Was that so much to ask?

Apparently, it was.

Chapter 14

Sean

THE WIND HOWLS through the trees outside, making it hard to sleep. He's been awake here or there throughout the night, anxiously checking his watch because Kate has put it in his head that someone is out there. He didn't truly believe it until today, when he found the footprints.

Though he could never tell her that – it would just cause a panic.

His wristwatch says it's a little past two in the morning when he's fully awake. His head is filled with worry as he knows that if the killer really did want to break in, he would have to be the man who faced him. Sean was never much of a fighter, but that didn't make him a coward. In fact, every fight he'd ever been in had been to protect others, even if he knew he'd lose. So when it comes to protecting his family, he'll do absolutely anything.

He gives up trying to sleep, climbing off the uncomfortable wooden chair and putting the fire poker on the side. Every night would be like this until they leave, barely sleeping and being ready to fight if it comes to it.

When he pours himself a glass of water, there's a tapping at the opposite window. Sean drops the glass. It hits the inside of the sink with a deafening smash. He spins around to watch the window. The curtains are closed, but there's a gap in between.

How has he been so careless?

Without hesitation, he grabs the fire poker and faces his fears. His shoes are on his feet in seconds before he heads outside and locks the door, taking the key with him. Nobody is going to get in while he investigates the sound.

Nobody.

The fierce wind takes his breath away, the harsh cold gnawing at his skin. The sweat on his chest and back only makes it worse, but he pays it no mind. Sean grips the poker tight and creeps around the exterior of the cottage, expecting someone to lunge at him.

Nobody does, but that doesn't mean nobody

was here. On the window where he heard the knocking is a handprint, smudging as it reaches the fingers. There's not a doubt in his mind that the killer was here, watching through the break in the curtains. It strikes fear deep into his heart because Kate is right to be afraid.

They should *all* be afraid.

Just like when he failed to report the footprints, Sean wants to minimise Kate's concerns. She knows the killer is out here, so there's no need for additional panic. He uses the bottom of his T-shirt to wipe the handprint off the glass, then does another lap of the perimeter.

The neighbours' cottage looks like a dead house, the lights off and a small patio lantern creaking as it swings in the wind. He wonders if he should warn Frank and Jeanie about their experiences, and maybe he will. Just not until it sounds less absurd.

There's nothing left to do but return to his guard post. Reaching for the key in his pyjama pocket, Sean rushes for the door to get out of the icy breeze, desperate to seek warmth even after such a short amount of time.

That's when he hears a heavy footstep among the trees.

'Is someone there?' he says, his voice carried by the wind.

He waits and waits, raw fear seizing him as he prepares to fight for his life.

And for the lives of those inside.

Chapter 15

Now

My eyes shoot open in the middle of the night. I'm certain I heard knocking, but could that be my insecure mind playing tricks on me? It doesn't matter either way because I'm awake now, and there's no chance of getting back to sleep until I know for sure.

I slowly climb off the floor, my body suffering from the pain of sleeping on hardwood. It's normal for someone in their mid-thirties, but that doesn't make it any more comfortable. I check on Hayden, who is snoring in the soft little way he does.

Then I move to the window for a look.

There's nothing but moonlit trees outside. Even if I squint – which is harder to do when my eyes are threatening to close under the strain of fatigue – there are only dead branches getting lashed around all over the place by harsh winds.

Suddenly, a figure moves past.

I drop the curtain and take a step back, wanting to gasp. But there's no breath in my body. My arms have goosebumps, a trickle of terror running up and down my back. There's no option but to leave Hayden, heading into the hall for Sean.

But he's gone.

My deepest fears are coming to life. The killer is here, but Sean isn't. I quickly notice the poker is gone. What does that mean? Has Sean gone out somewhere? Has the killer taken him, punishing him for my own sins – killing another man I love simply because I identified him last time? All of these questions are hurting my head, but they don't numb me just yet.

I act fast, turning off all the lights so my silhouette can't be seen from outside. I notice one of the curtains has a gap in it, which I immediately pull shut. I'm all alone now, facing nothing but darkness and doing so without Sean. I also have a son to protect.

That's all it takes for me to grab a knife from the kitchen block. I cower down in the corner by the cupboards, the knife gripped tight in my shaking, sweat-slicked hand as I wait in the dead of night. Sean has to come back to me – he *has* to – because I don't know what I would do in a world where he's not here to protect us.

I just know I wouldn't last long.

I've become one with my hiding place in the dark, the knife pointed outwards so as to ward off anyone who dares to come at me. Each painful second seems to stretch on for an eternity because I could be here all night. Every anxiety-inducing tick of the second hand on my watch strengthens my fear and weakens my knees.

What am I supposed to do?

Minutes go by. It feels like hours. There's movement outside – a silhouette gliding by. The killer is here for me, and I don't know whether to hide or run. I'm frozen, paralysed by the sheer horror of my past coming back to get me. I hold the knife closer, knowing full well I might not ever use it. A thud hits the front door. A little yelp escapes my lips.

Then I recognise it. It's the sound of a key in the door. Is it Sean, or does the killer have a copy?

My mind flickers back to the night he came in here, and we still don't know if we locked the door that night. It's a carelessness I'll never have again.

The key has turned, the lock with it. A blast of cold shoots in and reaches the kitchen. I can't see the door because the island is in the way, but I know I'm no longer alone. The footsteps creep into the cottage. My body goes rigid with horror, all my senses flaring off at once. I wait in the dark, knowing that if the killer goes towards Hayden's bedroom, then I have no choice but to attack. Do I really have it in me?

The figure reappears, approaching the chair that Sean has been using to sit in. He stops there, lurking in the blank room while the knife in my hand wavers. I think about doing it – about scrambling to my feet and attacking while screaming at the top of my lungs.

A switch sounds. Light floods the room. I freeze as Sean stands beside the chair, the poker still clutched in his hand. I can barely believe my luck, almost feeling stupid for how much I panicked. I drop the knife, clambering to my feet and rushing for him. When he spots me, he instantly drops the poker, opens his arms, and holds me tight, kissing my head as I bawl helplessly into his chest.

'There, there,' he says. 'It's nothing to worry about.'

'I thought you left me,' I say in a pathetic, weeping tone.

'Never.'

We stand like that forever. Sean doesn't move until the tears stop. Even then, he's gently rubbing my back because he knows that's how to calm me. There's no judgement from him whatsoever – he knows I'm rattled, and he knows why.

'What's going on?' says a curious, childlike voice.

Hayden has woken up in all the drama, and there's no way we're telling him the truth. Sean lets go of me. I turn my back away from my son so he can't see me cry while Sean talks to him in the most soothing tone.

'Your mum cut herself on a glass,' he lies. 'Go back to bed, mate.'

'Will she be okay?'

'Of course. It's just the smallest finger. She won't miss it.'

Hayden chuckles slightly. I hear the patter of his footsteps, followed by the clicking of the bedroom door. There's no way I'm spending the night away from him. I just need to clean up my teary face before he sees it. I don't want him to worry.

'Where were you?' I ask Sean when we're alone.

'I thought I heard a noise, so I went to investigate.'

'Did you find anything?'

'I thought so at first, but then... no.'

There's a little comfort in knowing I'm not the only one feeling spooked, but it doesn't change the fact that my husband's killer *is* out there somewhere. It's an undeniable fact. It makes me feel so uncomfortable that I can't stand still. I begin to pace the cottage, circling the island, the living room, then reversing my route, all while chewing on my nails.

'I don't want to be here,' I tell Sean.

Sean lowers himself into his guard chair. 'That's understandable.'

'No, I mean I want to leave. Sooner than we're supposed to.'

'We talked about this. There's no way to get back. Not safely anyway.'

'Do you think we're safe *here*?'

There's nothing he can say to that, though his mouth does open briefly like he wants to speak. When he goes silent, I follow suit and fall into deep thought. I've never felt so isolated in all my life. And to think, I initially considered that a good thing.

'What do you suppose we do?' Sean asks.

'Anything. Literally anything.'

'We could head next door and see if they'll protect us.'

'We've had this conversation.'

'And we need to have it again!'

The way Sean looks at me then, I wonder if he still loves me. If I were him, I wouldn't.

'I'm sorry, I didn't mean to snap,' I tell him. 'It's just that we're talking about our lives here. You must be worried, too. You can't deny it. Even you went outside when you heard a noise. Doesn't that tell you there's a cause for concern?'

Sean rubs his chin, his elbow propped on his knees as he stares at the floor. 'It's normal to be worried in a situation like this,' he says in a calm voice, probably hoping I'll match his tone. 'I'm open to the conversation, but maybe we should get some rest and talk it over when we're a little less exhausted. And calmer.'

I stop pacing, my arms now folded across my chest. Is it cold in here, or is that my panic talking? Whichever it is, I try to calm down because Sean is putting in that same effort. The least I can do is approach this rationally.

'Okay,' I tell him. 'We'll discuss it in the morning.'

After thanking him and saying goodnight, I head towards Hayden's room. My hand barely touches the handle before Sean tells me to wait. I turn and meet his gaze, and suddenly, it's so reassuring that I almost feel safe.

'I'll be watching out for you. Just relax and get some sleep.'

I nod and then enter the room, appreciating him so much for looking out for us. The thing is, he could sit there all night with a shotgun in his lap, but it still wouldn't change the fact that the killer is coming for me. That's why I watch the window all night, staring up at it from my place on the floor as the wind makes the cottage creek.

How is anyone supposed to sleep like this?

Maybe I'll ask Hayden in the morning.

. . .

NEXT MORNING, I find the killer has destroyed my appetite just like he once destroyed my life. Now I'm sitting at the island with a spoon in my hand, dunking it into a bowl of Cheerios. I can think of nothing worse than letting them near my uneasy stomach.

Hayden is in his room, lounging on the bed with one of those animal adventure books he seems to devour. The door is open so we can keep an ear out for him, but there's enough distance that Sean and I can speak in private if we keep our voices low. He touches my hand.

'Are you ready to talk about it?' he asks, stood up but leaning over the island.

I've been preparing for this moment all night. Not only to talk about the logistics of getting the hell out of here but also to explain the killer's hate for me – to finally reveal a secret I've been keeping from my boyfriend all this time. If he learns about this, at least he'll understand the extent the killer will go to just to finish me off.

'We should leave,' I say simply.

'Kate, you know we can't—'

'I'm not saying it's possible, but there's a pretty good reason to.'

'Yeah, I know. The killer is—'

'Can you just let me talk for a second? This is hard to say.'

Sean softens but lets go of my hand. He heads down the hall to check if Hayden is still distracted, then returns to me. He pulls out a stool. 'Okay. No judgement here. Whatever you need to get off your chest, I'm here for you.'

I inhale slowly, drawing in a long breath that may not be enough to steady me. This secret has been locked away inside me for so long that I'm not quite sure how to feel. It will reveal the worst part of my soul, and it might make Sean question his entire opinion of me.

But it has to be said.

'The killer is here because he wants to see me dead,' I say. 'Punished, even. If you cut out the how and the where, you'll be left with the why. That's what I need to tell you about. Because it goes deeper than you ever thought, and...'

I pause, drop the spoon into the bowl, then push it all away from me. There's not a chance in hell I'm going to keep food down after this. I can count on one hand the number of times I've been this nervous. Two of those times were on this trip.

The other...

'I did something wrong. Meaning he has every

right to hate me. What you do know is that he killed my husband and ruined my life, but you don't know the real truth. That he didn't deserve to get hunted by the police all this time.'

Sean says nothing. He just looks at me, the green in his eyes searching for the truth. There's nothing but patience and understanding, but that doesn't mean he won't hate me after this. Now may even be the last time he'll ever love me.

But I have to tell him.

'This is what happened the night Nick was murdered...'

Chapter 16
Then

OUR THREE-YEAR-OLD SON *had crept into our bed in the middle of the night, making things very difficult for 'Father Christmas' to place a range of gifts under our tree. Thankfully, my Ryan-related woes had kept me up for hours anyway, so as soon as I heard Hayden's breath get heavy and saw him snuggle his dad for comfort, I sneaked out of the room and got to work.*

There was so much to be done. The wrapped presents had to be taken from our locked walk-in wardrobe and set in their rightful place under the pines. Stockings needed filling and – since we had no chimney – set down at the end of our bed. Nick and I would wake up and feign surprise, encouraging Hayden to become as excited about the day as we seemed to be. He was now at that age where he started to know what was going on.

Later, that would turn out to be a bad thing.

When all was in place, I checked the clock. It was exactly five in the morning, and I didn't feel like going back to bed, so I took to our balcony and watched London wake up on the streets below. Vans were coming and going, the early risers out jogging and a lone woman performing the walk of shame in a revealing dress and one broken high heel. I was so glad those years were behind me, but now I had bigger problems to deal with.

Because today was the day.

When I was ready to face the music, I checked my phone. There were multiple messages from Ryan, the most recent of which was sent only an hour ago. I could hardly believe he was up already, committing hard to the idea of he and I in the sack together.

It wasn't going to happen.

My mother had been right in saying Nick deserved to know, but I was in control of the situation. If my family was about to break, I would do it on my own terms. Besides, I had too much respect for Nick to let him find out from someone else. I just needed one more day, and that was exactly what I told Ryan when I typed the text.

I've decided we'll have sex. But I need one more day.

Even though it was just my way of stalling, I still felt sick to actually put those words over to him. I waited in the cold, hugging my own torso as I stared dead-eyed at the skyline. London was beautiful when it was dark out, but I failed to see the beauty that morning.

Other, more important things were happening.

My phone buzzed, and I looked at it instantly. The message Ryan had sent back left me scared and breathless. Persistent as ever, it didn't look like I was going to buy myself enough time to tell Nick the truth.

It read:

Today.

My thumbs moved of their own accord as I dug in my proverbial heels. There was no way I would let him dictate what I did with my body. I was hoping the threat of losing his chance might make him change his ways, so I tried another reply:

Tomorrow or not at all.

As soon as it was sent, I went back inside. When I shut the balcony door, the chill air lingered for a few moments longer. I shivered, grabbed a blanket off the sofa, and wrapped it around me. It felt coarse against my skin and smelled a bit musty, but I didn't care.

Once more, my phone buzzed. I read the text and wished I hadn't. Ryan was being even more stubborn than I was, and I didn't know what to do. I stood there in my living room with the phone shaking in my hand, a nauseating sensation making me dizzy.

Today.

That was all it said. It needn't have said more. It looked like I wasn't destined to get my own way, and time could not be bought. I replied to Ryan, telling him it would have to be late at night because I was spending the day with my family. I hoped he'd be rational and see how hard it was to slip away from my family on Christmas Day.

When he told me it had to be in the afternoon or he'd spill my secret, my mind was made up. I would have to enjoy Christmas morning, exchanging gifts with giddy smiles. We would eat dinner at two, pulling crackers and telling the awful jokes that fell from the centres. Then, when Hayden went down for his nap, I would tell Nick the truth.

This was it, whether I liked it or not.

He would find out today.

I ENJOYED *the morning with my family, pretty much certain it wasn't going to last long. It surprised me that not only did we make it to the afternoon, but there was still no word from Ryan. Had he been bluffing all along?*

It got me thinking that maybe our secret had been safe this whole time. Ryan was Nick's best friend, so spilling the beans on our kiss would be a great loss for him, too. Not that it really changed anything in the long run.

I still had to tell Nick.

Come late afternoon on the last good Christmas, we had Home Alone 2 *on in the background as we all sat around to play Hayden's new board game. It was like Mouse Trap, except we were capturing monsters using less strategic means. We all had to wear gloves, clawing our way at plastic moulds of the most menacing, cartoonish creatures I'd ever laid eyes on. We were having fun. Nick and I were laughing as Hayden beamed the whole time.*

Until there was a knock on the door.

'I'll get it,' I said, starting to stand up.

But Nick was on his feet before me, rushing for the door. I sat back, trying to relax while Hayden made up his own rules and started climbing over the sofa in his monster gloves. I took mine off and tried listening out for who was at the door. But Macaulay Culkin was panicking in a hotel room on the TV, and the remote was in Nick's pocket.

At least I could hear the door open. A soft mumble, but that was it. If that was Ryan, and if he'd come here to explain all that had happened – incriminating himself, too, of course – then I wanted to enjoy the last few happy moments of this day. I spun around and crawled towards Hayden, pretending I was a larger monster that ate the smaller ones. Hayden giggled and ran around the room, his delighted squeal like music to my ears.

Over time, I forgot about Nick and Ryan at the

door. I loved our son, and seeing him this happy trumped any potential threat from the outside. We continued playing, Hayden claiming that he was now a monster who dieted exclusively on chocolate. Even though it was Christmas, I wasn't ready to give him sugar just yet. He was already bouncing off the walls.

When I stopped for a quick breather, I looked at the clock. Macaulay's visitors were fleeing the room on the TV, and Nick had been gone for some time. I called out to him, asking if all was okay. His failure to respond concerned me, but I thought maybe he hadn't heard me because he was deep in conversation.

About me, probably.

After a couple more minutes, I thought it might be time to investigate – to face the music, if you will. I told Hayden to wait for just a moment and that I would be right back. He asked again for chocolate, and because I was tired of telling him no, I promised he could have a small piece in a minute if he was good.

Meanwhile, Mummy had to check on something.

I saw the blood long before I saw the body. It oozed away from the hall and began to trail into the living room. Thankfully, Hayden was distracted by the film on the TV, which left me to suffer alone as I rounded the corner.

Nick's body was revealed inch by inch, time seeming to slow down. My hand covered my mouth, but I didn't remember raising it. My husband was on the floor, the front door wedged open by his lifeless foot. His eyes – God, I'll never forget those shocked, desperate eyes, frozen in time while begging for help – were bloodshot, his mouth stuck in an agonised expression.

I couldn't move. I couldn't breathe. My whole life had been taken away while I was playing silly games in the other room. Hayden's father had been murdered, and he was none the wiser. It took a while for any of this to register, but when it did, it hit hard.

That was the worst moment of my life.

'CHOCOLATE, MUMMY,' Hayden said from the other room. 'Chocolate.'

How long had I been standing there? It was hard to say. Could have been seconds, minutes, or an hour. That's the thing about trauma – it completely wrecks your ability to think straight. It didn't even occur to me that I had to do something about it.

Not until Hayden started walking my way.

I spun around and scooped him up, holding him close so he couldn't see I was crying. Something like that would only open him up to more questions, and right then, I was struggling to find my breath. All I could do was shush him and carry him into his bedroom, sitting him on the bed and telling him I had to go and do something real quick.

'But I can come with you,' he said, fighting against me.

'No, honey, you have to stay. Just for a little while.'

The tears started to flow. 'Can I have chocolate?'

I took a few short steps into the kitchen and grabbed a Cadbury selection box from the worktop, then took it back and put it in his lap, tearing open the cardboard and letting all the packages fall out. I then quickly opened a few of them at random, my hands quivering under the stress of it all. 'Here, have all the chocolate you want,' I said. 'Just stay in your room.'

Hayden's room had a lock on it. It had been there when we moved in, and the key stayed in the door. I used it for the first and last time because letting him see his father's dead body was far more cruel than keeping him prisoner for an hour or so. I'm not proud of it, but I wasn't really thinking logically.

After all, my husband was dead.

I checked Nick wasn't breathing, then checked again as if the result might differ. It didn't, but I couldn't accept it. I called 999 and asked for an ambulance, police, anyone who could help because Nick had been murdered, and there was blood all over the place. While I did this, the operator told me to remain calm as I paced up and down our grand living room. People were on their way, I was told, so I stood on the balcony and waited in the cold, refreshing air for lights and sirens to appear on our street. It felt like they were taking their precious time.

Who knows how long it really took?

There was a sudden bang behind me, but over time, I began to realise that it wasn't behind me at all but coming from the main door on the ground floor. A hooded figure fled the scene, strutting up the street like his life depended on it. I held the phone to my ear but didn't speak a word, mostly because I was too dazed to process my thoughts.

The hooded man reached the end of the street. He turned and looked up at me. I'd never felt as vulnerable as I did right then, gazing down at my husband's killer. You're probably wondering who it was, or you might have even guessed that it was Ryan, taking my husband's life out of sheer jealousy in a psychotic moment of rage.

That was what I told the police, too – that Ryan had killed Nick.

But the truth was, I didn't see his face. I've thought about it non-stop ever since, almost certain that he was the culprit. I mean, who else could it have been? Ryan was supposed to be coming over to unveil the big secret, and this was so obviously a premeditated murder. If it had been someone else, I might have been surprised when a note later appeared on my pillow, but for all I know, Ryan had been falsely accused.

Who wouldn't be angry about that?

The investigation began immediately, but what hurts me the most is that Nick died quite possibly because of something I did, and he didn't even know why. I sometimes think about his final moments and wonder if the truth had been whispered to him during the attack. Then I come back down to earth and realise that there was no proof it was Ryan.

I had given his name to the police based on an educated guess.

Justice was never served.

Chapter 17

Now

I DON'T KNOW exactly what I was expecting from Sean, but I definitely didn't expect him to get off his stool and wrap his arms around me. Not only is he a policeman who was involved in the case, but he's heard me say multiple times that I saw Ryan leaving the building.

His breath is warm, his embrace even warmer. I close my eyes and lean into him, letting the soft scent of his cologne make me feel right at home. The tears are starting to come, but for once, they're not of self-pity.

This time, it's self-hate.

'Why didn't you tell me any of this before?' he asks.

'I was worried it might get you in trouble.'

'Why would it?'

'Because you have to keep it a secret. That can't be easy for a cop.'

He eases off me, and I use the opportunity to reach for my glass of water. It feels like I'm washing down a nail because of all the dryness in my throat. I didn't realise I was this nervous about confessing the truth. I realise, of course, there's still a very small chance Sean may have to report this. It proves I lied in my statement, after all.

Hayden pops his head through the bedroom door and looks around. When he sees me crying, he takes a couple of steps towards me, his thumb wedged into the book in his hand so he doesn't lose his place. I see genuine concern as he furrows his brow.

'Mum, are you all right?'

'She's fine, mate,' Sean says. 'Just give us a minute?'

Hayden nods and then backs away, stealing one final glance before he disappears and closes the door. We're alone again, only now I'm a worse person than before. At least I must be in Sean's eyes. He takes his seat back on the stool and looks across at me, holding my attention with eyes so green they remind me of a meadow.

'Let me ask you something,' he says. 'Do you still think it's Ryan who killed Nick?'

I pause because there's a seriousness in his tone that makes me feel a little like I'm being interviewed. It encourages me to give my most honest answer. 'I'm prepared to accept that it could've been someone else, but I strongly believe it was Ryan.'

'May I ask why?'

I've been lying for so many years that I almost say it's because I *saw* him. But as I just confessed, all I got a glimpse of was a dark hoodie with black jeans. It could have been anyone, so I choose my words carefully.

'Doesn't it just seem too coincidental?' I ask. 'He was planning on coming over when the killer arrived. I never heard from Ryan again, even though he'd been pressing me to sleep with him. Nobody has seen him since, and that means he hasn't given an alibi for that day. Is there proof that it was him? Absolutely not. But you can't deny it makes sense.'

'Okay.' Sean breathes deeply, then cups his mouth with stress. 'So let's say it's the killer who left that note on our pillow. Do you think that's Ryan?'

'What do you mean?'

'Well, you just said there's a chance Ryan didn't do it. So doesn't that mean whoever *did* do it is up here in the woods somewhere? Either that or Ryan hates you for accusing him and has come up here to make you pay.'

I hate that it didn't even cross my mind, but he's right. Supposing Ryan wasn't the killer, he'd have every incentive to come after me. I mean, the accusation alone destroyed his life, so of course he'd want revenge. Then again, the *real* killer could have his own motive.

A brand-new conundrum has just opened up.

'Sorry if that's making you overthink,' Sean says calmly.

'No, it's fine. I'm just worried what you must think of me.'

'Why?'

'Because it's possible I falsely accused someone of murder.'

'For what it's worth, it very likely was Ryan who killed Nick. Given everything I know about the case, it would make perfect sense. It wouldn't hold up in court, but it's logical.' Sean sighs, then leans across the island. 'But there is something else.'

I stare deeply into his eyes, searching for a truth before I hear it. A thousand things could come out of his mouth, but when he finally speaks, I can barely believe what I'm hearing.

'I already knew,' he says. 'I knew you didn't see Ryan that night. Let me explain.'

I REALISE I'm holding my breath, feeling a strange whirlwind of curiosity and anger. I've been holding onto that secret for so long, letting it build up inside me like a storming tempest, knocking and thrashing me, making me feel lost at sea. Sean looks down at his hands as he begins to talk, and all I can do is listen while my heart punches against my ribs.

'You know I was one of the first on the scene,' he says. 'Obviously, we didn't know each other then, and you later admitted you didn't even recognise me. For all intents and purposes, I was just a man in the room as you explained to the detectives what happened.

'I remember it like it was yesterday. You were sitting on the sofa with Hayden in your arms, trying to distract him with toys so he didn't have to hear your side of the story. I didn't like it, so I knelt down and spoke to him, then lured him away. You went on to explain how you'd seen the killer and that it was Ryan. What you didn't know – and I wasn't about to announce that you were lying, but I knew – was that the man leaving the building wore a hood.

'But how did I know? Simple: like I said, I was first on the scene. My partner and I were stuck in traffic when he got the radio call. We were to stop outside your flat on Marylebone and investigate a call about a murder. We parked right away, and the second I got out of the car, my eyes were drawn to a man storming down the street with his hood up. That night was cold, but it wasn't wet, so he stuck out like a sore thumb. I didn't think much of it until I went inside and heard your story. It just didn't match what I'd seen.'

As Sean talks, my hands are starting to shake. It's like I'm about to go to prison for falsely accusing someone, or at the very least be punished for obstructing the course of justice. But I couldn't help letting him speak, each word hitting me like a battering ram.

'There was security in the lobby,' he goes on. 'Not a physical person but a security camera that caught the comings and goings. I was a part of the team who had to review it for legal purposes, and all we saw was that hooded man. People were starting to talk about how you might not have been one hundred per cent truthful in your statement, and then my colleagues began to speculate.

'But here's where the problem lies: I found myself drawn to you. Call it pity or empathy, I don't care which, but I really felt for you after the story you'd given. It made complete sense that this Ryan fella had killed your husband, so I knew something had to be done.

'That's why I stole the tape.'

I was stunned, speechless. The detectives told me some evidence had gone missing, but I didn't know Sean was involved in any of that. Now my mouth has gone dry, and I can barely get a word out because my perfect boyfriend has broken the law.

And lied about it.

'You might hate me for what I did, Kate, but I did it to protect you. My colleagues were talking about how you lied, one or two of them intending to prove it. I understood why you'd made your accusation, so I took the tape, crushed it, then threw it into the Thames. It will never be recovered, and that only serves to benefit you.'

'But...' I couldn't get my words out. Of all the

things I knew about Sean, I was certain he wasn't a liar. Now that seems to have come undone as one major lie has been held back this whole time. Not only that, but he let me feel guilty all this time, making me hold my secret about what happened on the night of Nick's murder.

I feel all different kinds of things, but I just can't bring myself to cry. I feel ashamed of what I've done, shocked at what Sean went through to keep me out of trouble, and angry that he kept it from me this whole time. It's starting to feel like there's not a single person on this earth I can trust. What shortly follows is a numb, sick feeling. My stomach curdles, my tongue dry as sandpaper. I can't even look at Sean.

'I lied for *you*,' he says.

By then, my world is spinning, making me feel woozy. I'm on my feet in the bat of an eye, rushing towards the kitchen sink so I can throw up without making a mess. My chest is tight, and Sean comes to rub my back, calming me.

That's when I shrug him off and tell him to leave me alone.

Right now, I can't stand the sight of him.

. . .

AFTER CLEANING up the mess I made, all I want is to go outside and get some air. But then it hits me that I can't. The outside world is off limits for as long as the killer is out there. I need to get away from Sean – to process this in private while I taste my own tears.

'Can I get you something?' he asks from behind.

'Just leave me alone for a bit, will you?'

To be fair to him, he gives me what I need. I drink some water, but not much because it won't settle, and then I head to the bedroom and try my very best not to close the door. It's hard to understand exactly what I should be feeling. Sean isn't a bad person – he only did one bad thing, but even that was to protect me. I suppose I should be grateful, but more than anything, it just feels like I've been lied to this whole time.

Then there's the guilt.

Sean's not the bad guy here. I am. As much as I automatically put the blame on him for my current sorry state, it's my own wrongdoings that are making me sick. Not only did I accuse someone of murder and lie in my statement, but I also kept it from Sean the whole time. Some might say that was the smart thing to do, given that he's a cop, but he's more than that.

I love him.

Which only makes it hurt more.

I lie face down on the bed, letting the tears dampen the cotton. I've got so much anger building up inside me that I need to walk it off. But I can't leave Hayden alone, and I just know I might not return from that head-clearing stroll. I'm stuck here – we all are – and all because of me. Because I was too fast to point the finger, and now we're all paying for it.

A knock raps upon the door. Sean enters, places another glass of water on the bedside table, then tells me he's sorry. I roll onto my side and look at the bare trees outside the window. They look like wooden arms, coming to grab me and take me away – to punish me for the things I did wrong. It's not logical, I know that, but I hate Sean right now.

I hate *him* for what *I* did.

'I'm sorry,' he says.

Then, before I can reply, the door is shut, and I'm alone.

What have I done?

Chapter 18

Then

THE POLICE HAD THEIR REPORT. *I'd told them* *everything I knew about Ryan and why I was* *apparently so certain he'd killed Nick. Of course,* *Scotland Yard had their own theories about what* *might have happened to him, so I was put through* *the wringer just like anyone else might have been.* *Like they say, more often than not, it's the spouse.*

But this wasn't a domestic murder case. People *knew it, I knew it, and – most of all – the media* *knew it. I was starting to become very infamous all* *over England, but it was one of those blink-and-* *you'll-miss-it affairs. I loved Nick. It was obvious I* *could never hurt him.*

It's not like the evidence against Ryan wasn't *strong either. The police had records of my text* exchanges with him, which soon got leaked to the press. It was hard to keep any sort of personal life after that. I hated it, mostly because Hayden was starting to grow up in the public eye. Nobody should wish that on their child.

By the time a single month had passed, the media was starting to accept me as innocent. As well they should because Nick's death was horrifically traumatising for me. My appetite had gone – I was losing weight fast, barely able to put together a meal for my own son. The flat was a mess, and things were getting out of hand. There were dishes sitting in the sink from a month ago. Every surface was coated in a thick layer of dust. It was a dark, bleak place, as if misery had swept in and replaced all the fun and joy we'd had as a family.

I couldn't even go near the door because it would trigger that awful memory again.

Most of my time was spent on the sofa, staring numbly at the TV, both morbidly curious and anxiously fearful of the next news report. Hayden was playing on the carpet by himself one morning, making his own fun, while my heart started to stutter as the news began.

Ryan was back in the spotlight. My name was being officially cleared, and it was about time. It *was shocking just how much I wanted to see him suffer for what he might not have even done in the first place. I had considered that – because Ryan had gone on the run and not been heard from since, even by his closest family – maybe he really was the killer.*

On tonight's programme, they were inter-viewing the people he'd worked with, all of whom were in the sales department for Jaguar. Not on the showroom floor, as Ryan had always been quick to point out, but selling to the showrooms. What was the difference exactly? He'd always said it was the pay, but I'd seen his flat. It wasn't much.

Another lie from Nick's best friend.

The reporter mentioned something about a documentary being in the works, which meant I would probably get bombarded by interviewers all over again. I didn't see what set this particular murder apart from your usual London type. Again, I suspected it was just the media selling tickets to a show they'd created from their own little spin.

I switched off the TV and stared at Hayden. He rolled a wooden car around the carpet and seemed perfectly content. It was only a matter of time until the waterworks started, however, so I enjoyed the moment of peace while it lasted.

It didn't take long for that to reach an abrupt end.

As soon as Hayden found the Formula One car he and Nick used to play with all the time, he snatched it up and looked around the room. I knew my calmness had ended, but I didn't have the strength to do anything about it. I was still a broken widow, finding even the easiest tasks a great challenge to overcome.

But this was by no means easy.

The routine had begun as soon as that toy car had been located. Hayden's eyes were focused as he frowned, slowly growing more and more frustrated as he couldn't find his father. As was becoming a habit, he then locked eyes with me, looking lost and afraid.

'Dadda,' he said.

I didn't know what to say because I wasn't sure if it was right or wrong to tell him his dadda wasn't coming back. I felt like the worst mother in the world as I pulled out a cushion and pressed it against one ear. Then I lay down on the sofa, which had been my resting place for so many days and nights that my petite body was starting to ache.

Hayden's lower lip caved outwards.

Then the howling began.

It started with a long whine that seemed to go on and on. Then he took a breath, still staring me dead in the eye, and let out the longest, most ear-piercing scream I'd ever heard. I closed my eyes just so I didn't have to look at him while he yelled the building down. I felt a raging inferno inside me, conflicting emotions breaking me little by little.

Yes, *I thought,* you want your dadda. I want your dadda. We all want your dadda to come back, but he's not coming back because his creep of a best friend stabbed him multiple times in the stomach. *I squeezed my eyes shut tighter and begged for this to be over because Hayden's tears encouraged my tears, and there was nothing I could do to bring Nick back to his son.*

It went on until I could no longer stand it. I loved Hayden, but I felt completely lost as a mother. How the hell was anyone supposed to handle this? How was I supposed to explain the concept of life and death to a three-year-old?

Nick would have known how.

It made me want to curl up more, but my temper grew and grew like a fire in a dry forest. I'm ashamed to say this, but I snapped. Without even thinking, I hurled the cushion across the room. It hit the TV, the zip leaving a scratch on the screen.

There wasn't time to assess the damage because I was already scooping Hayden up and carrying him to his room, placing him on the bed and then shutting the door.

The screaming continued, even if it was more muffled. I leaned with my back against the door and looked up, as if asking God to save me from this nightmare. I was neglecting my son because I didn't know what to do. Hayden stayed in there, banging and knocking against the wall or the wood of his bed or... something I wasn't sure of.

It took me some time to realise it wasn't him.

The knocking was coming from the front door. I'd been avoiding texts and calls and visitors since the day Nick died, but I found myself rushing for the door just for a break from all the screaming. While I unhooked the latch, I began to worry that it might be a journalist looking for the inside scoop.

But then I saw who it was, and I didn't know how to feel.

She was about to feel either very sympathetic or very ashamed.

THERE WAS no hiding the questionable look on her aged face as she stood at my front door. She pulled *off her gloves, her eyes not leaving mine as she scowled. She suddenly looked like one of those old ladies from the forties, all fur-coated and rich-looking.*

Not to mention condescending.

'What's all that screaming about?' she asked. 'Aren't you taking care of your own son?'

I sighed and opened the door wider for her to come in. She sniffed as she breezed past me, likely noticing I hadn't even been taking care of myself. It'd been two weeks since my last shower. My hair was dry, my skin smelling like old rubber. Staying clean was the least of my worries, but I at least tried to sound like I didn't hate to see her.

'Hi, Mum,' I said, closing the door.

She didn't stick around to ask my questions — she simply followed the wailing into the bedroom, where she found Hayden red-faced and thrashing around on his bed. I cupped my hand over my mouth and lowered my head with indignity while she studied me. When that was finally over, she headed into the room and magically stopped the crying instantly.

I didn't know what she was saying, and I never would, but it didn't really matter. My mother had always been a master with kids. All kids except for her own daughter, that was, and my current state of disgusting, bitter loneliness was proof of that.

While she worked her charm in Hayden's bedroom, I went into the kitchen and put the kettle on. There were no clean mugs among the pile of dishes, so I took a used one and swilled it out with warm water, preparing a coffee for my royal visitor. This was one thing she'd been super strict on as she'd raised me: I must always have drinks waiting for my guests.

Even if I didn't know they were coming, apparently.

As I poured the coffee, my mother found me in the kitchen. Hayden was now playing happily in the living room again, his detonation time now wound back and beginning its countdown all over again. I always marvelled at her ability to do that.

If only that would work on me.

'I know what you're thinking,' I said, putting the coffee in her hand and then passing through to the living room. She followed me in, where I plunked down onto the sofa and hugged my knees to my chest. 'Spare me the judgement though. It's not welcome here.'

Still silent, she sat in the armchair across from me, picking up a crumpled magazine and making a poor effort not to turn her nose up at the mess as she placed it on the coffee table. When she finally spoke, her tone was surprisingly calm.

'You're neglecting your son,' she said.

'I know that.'

'And you're not inspired to fix it?'

'I've just lost my husband, Mum. Things aren't so clear-cut.'

Her eyes went to Hayden, who was handing her a plastic egg that she didn't know what to do with. She took it awkwardly, patted him on the head, then gave it back. Hayden stared at it for a second before wandering off again.

'You only needed to ask for help if you wanted it. Contrary to popular belief, I'm not a monster. As if talking to me might bring some almighty interference to your life, I suspect. You haven't even picked up your phone.'

'I've had things to do,' I said bluntly.

'Like what? Sulking?'

'Come on.'

'I'm just saying, you're so wrapped up in losing your husband that you aren't dealing with Hayden's needs. He's lost a father, you know.' My mother sighed and then crossed the room to sit beside me. 'Do you remember when we lost your father?'

'How can I forget?'

'Do you also remember how I reacted?'

I nodded because speaking would only open a floodgate of nasty words. I remember losing my dad very well because my mum went travelling to take her mind off it all. She'd left me with a nanny she barely knew, grieving in the arms of a stranger.

'I'm well aware of what I did,' she said. 'It haunts me every day. It most likely bothers you, too, and that's exactly what I'm trying to warn you about. Do you want Hayden to grow up thinking of you the same way you think of me?'

'What do I think of you, exactly?'

'Why don't you tell me?'

I sucked in a deep breath and let it out slowly, refusing to take the bait.

'It needn't be said,' she went on, 'but I know I could have done a better job at raising you. Affection never was my forte, but that doesn't mean you can't learn from my mistakes. When it comes to handling the loss of a loved one, in the very least.'

'I don't know what you expect from me,' I said. 'I know I'm failing. I just can't find the strength in me to get off the sofa for more than five minutes. I loved Nick so much, and now he's...' I stopped *myself before the tears came. She didn't need to see me cry.*

'Why don't I take Hayden?' she suggested. 'Just for a few days. On the condition that you get up, clean yourself, go out for a walk. Do whatever you need to do to start finding your new normal or whatever it is you kids say today.'

My hand went to my mouth, and I gnawed on my nails once again. For once in her life, my mother had a good idea and was offering to make herself useful for more than five minutes. It almost felt as though she knew what I was going through, which I suppose she did.

But could I leave Hayden for a few days at a time? I probably didn't have a choice because if I carried on this way, then who knew what might happen? Finally, I nodded and gave my mother the go-ahead to take over for a while.

It was the only way to not ruin my son.

Chapter 19

Now

Time to reflect is important. I had that and then some, feeling sorry for myself while locked away in that room. Just like when Nick died, I starve myself until the sun goes down, only sitting up when my stomach groans. But all of this self-pity is exhausting, which causes me to lie down again, practically just blinking before morning comes.

I can hear Hayden in the next room, banging around as he searches for cereal bowls. Sean is telling him to keep it down so I can get some rest, but I'm awake now. Which means I won't be going back to sleep. If I don't get up now, my only other option is to reflect on last night.

Trust me, I'm completely aware of how I

behaved last night. Sean doesn't deserve my anger. All he did was hide the evidence that proved I was a liar. Sure, it was morally wrong, but his intentions were good. I think I was simply lashing out because I made myself angry with the things I'd done. Sean didn't deserve to be treated like that.

I'll apologise today.

Some quiet talking makes my ears prick. I sit up on the bed again and peer through the window. There's a morning frost, the whole forest kissed by white. It's beautiful, but my attention is rather drawn to Frank and Jeanie, who are standing on their patio with steaming cups in their hands. Frank has his arm around Jeanie. They're both smiling.

Like Nick and I used to smile.

No. I kill that thought before it drags me back down. I must actually get up and do something if I'm to keep myself from moping around all day long. Grabbing a hoodie from the back of the make-up chair, I wish my family a good morning while speeding through the living room and out the door. I'm hoping to catch the neighbours before they go back inside.

The cold air takes my breath away. It was so toasty in the cottage that it didn't even occur to me how much the bitter winter might bite. I zip the hoodie up to my neck and hug myself, my frosty breath clouding in front of me while I shiver, making my way next door.

'Morning,' I say, making them startle. 'Sorry to scare you.'

'That's quite all right,' Jeanie says.

'I was wondering if I can talk to you about something serious.' I take a look at their concerned faces, then glance back at the cottage. Sean is twitching the net curtain in the kitchen, and I wonder if he thinks less of me for doing this.

But deep in my heart, I know it's right.

I tell them everything: about Nick and Ryan, the note, being followed in the woods, and so on. They listen patiently, trying to remain calm, but Jeanie's worry is plain to see. The mug in her hand is shaking quite violently. Until Frank takes it off her, then holds her hand.

'Thank you for telling us,' he says to me. 'It must have been a hard thing to do.'

'I said I recognised her,' Jeanie mumbles. 'From the news.'

Frank nods, then gives me a look like a concerned father. 'Are you okay?'

'Yes, I think so. It's just that this has turned into

a holiday from hell. We can't seem to do anything or go anywhere without looking over our shoulders. I just wanted to make you two aware of the danger and to ask if you might have seen someone.'

'I'm afraid not.' Frank looks around now like it might help. 'But we'll definitely let you know if we do. I don't sleep much in the night, so next time I wake up, I'll sit and watch the windows. Also, if you find yourself in trouble, don't you hesitate to come knocking. It's safer with the five of us than with just the three of you.'

'Thank you.'

I say goodbye and trudge back to the cottage, slipping and sliding in all the icy mud. Despite initial suspicion that our neighbours might have had something to do with the note, I realise now that it was merely paranoia. I'm coming out of my shell a little, gaining some much-needed clarity on the whole situation. So that's one uncomfortable situation down.

There's one more to go.

SEAN MEETS me at the door, reaching for my hand and looking into my eyes with the deepest sympathy. Even after I got upset and yelled at him, he's still looking after my needs. It just goes to show how much I acted out.

'Are you okay?' he says. 'I was worried you were leaving the forest.'

'Thankfully, I'm not stupid enough to even try it. Can we talk?'

He reaches inside and grabs two coats, handing one to me and sliding the other on himself. He tells Hayden to lock the door behind us and only open when he hears six knocks, explaining that we're just going to walk around the building. It's news to me, but I don't mind – the air is beautiful and refreshing, the smell of pine somehow warming me.

We begin a slow and careful stroll, avoiding the muddy sections and still keeping an eye on the windows as we pass them. I keep my head down in between, feeling pretty ashamed of the way I treated Sean last night.

'About our conversation,' I say, huffing out a big breath. 'I'm sorry I lost my temper with you. I think I was in defence mode because of the secret I let you in on, and it also made me feel like a scumbag. So when you told me you hid the evidence, I might have subconsciously thought of it as a place to put my anger.'

Sean puts an arm around me and pulls me tight. His body heat is so comforting, his touch making me relax instantly as we walk. 'You don't need to apologise to me. It was a strange conversation, both of us admitting to something bad.'

'That's just it. What you did wasn't that bad.'

'It's illegal. Tampering with evidence and so on.'

'But you did it for me.'

'That doesn't make it right.' It's Sean's turn to sigh, a burst of steam expelling into the air. He looks down, the usual smile missing from his expression. 'I feel awful about hiding that tape. Not a day goes by that I don't think about it. But if I could turn back time, I'd do the same thing over and over again.'

I go silent, thinking about what might have happened if he hadn't done what he'd done. The police would know I lied about seeing Ryan's face, and then the heat would be on me. Once the press gets hold of something like that, they never release their unforgiving grip. Even if I didn't end up in jail, my life would be ruined. Not to mention Hayden's.

'Thank you for doing what you did,' I say. 'And for keeping my secret.'

193

'Don't thank me. Just do me a favour and try not to beat yourself up about it. For what it's worth, it sounds like Ryan really did kill Nick. In a logical world, it would be easy to point the finger and condemn him for that. It's only because of the legal system that he's not behind bars right now. That, and the fact the police can't find him, I guess.'

'Which I see as an admission of guilt in itself.'

'Not necessarily.'

'What do you mean?'

'If you were accused of murder and the evidence was against you, would you stand there with your wrists held out, waiting for the handcuffs to be slapped on?'

I think about that, trying not to feel like Sean is jumping back and forth between sides. But he has a point, and I love that he's not afraid to voice it just for the sake of being fair. Being objective means a lot to him, and that makes sense, given that he's a policeman.

'You're probably right,' I say, stopping outside the window where Frank and Jeanie had been nearby only a couple of minutes ago. 'I do sometimes wonder if I was wrong, but Ryan pretty much set himself up for this. Sometimes I wish they would catch him just so I could hear his side of the story, you know?'

Sean nods, takes my hand, and tells me he knows. He takes me into his warm embrace, and now it feels like the dust has settled from my explosive reaction last night. We can go back to relaxing now. At least as much as possible while a killer is watching us. I just feel like there's less of a burden now that the secret has been shared. Sean is taking half of the weight for me, keeping the truth to himself without judgement.

Just like he's been doing this whole time.

THE REST of the day is filled with fun times *inside* the cottage. I trusted Sean to keep an eye on us, and he didn't once let down his guard. Even while we watch films and play board games, he keeps getting up to check the windows and peer through the small pane of glass at the top of the door. It's unsettling, like an intrusive reminder that we're being watched, but there's nothing to do except continue trying to have fun.

At least we're safe.

For now.

When bedtime comes, I tell Sean it might be

worth him catching up on a little sleep. I decided that if the killer hasn't broken down the door to try killing us yet, then he might not do it at all. Just a few short hours on the sofa might help, but he refuses it completely, insisting that his family rests while he waits, watching.

I immediately fall asleep on Hayden's bedroom floor, even though it's hard and cold. I've exhausted myself with all the worry, so within seconds, I'm dreaming that I'm back at the flat. Nick is still alive, and Hayden is eight years old, so he obviously survived the attack. That, or there never was one. Now it's all love and fun until there's a knock on the door. I don't open it because I know what will happen – that my husband will be taken away from me. So I sit there and stare as it slowly creeks open, whining on its hinge as the killer enters our home. I can't see his face, but I know it's Ryan. My rapid heartbeat proves it.

I shoot up from the floor, waking myself as I climb to my knees. My mind is still in a fog as my brain catches up to the fact I'm now in the real world. I watch Hayden and wonder why he stopped playing with Nick. Then it twigs, and I look at the window.

One second is all it takes to see it.

There's a shadow behind the curtain. There usually is, but this time, it looks different. Larger. Most of the time, I run over and open it, biting back my fear just to prove it's my imagination. I do the same this time, doing my best to ignore the queasy sensation. When I reach the window, I yank back the curtain to prove once again it's my imagination.

Except it isn't. Not this time. I gasp out loud as I see Ryan standing there, grinning at me in the dark with a large hunting knife in his hand. I step back, my heel landing on something hard. I cry in pain. Hayden suddenly wakes, and he must see what I see because he screams.

Ryan heads out of sight. I don't waste any time, quickly encouraging Hayden off the bed and out of the room. Sean stumbles to alertness at all the panicking, our heavy footsteps pounding up the hall. Hayden is crying, and I'm close to it.

'What is it?' Sean asks, leaping to his feet.

'Ryan! Outside!'

Without missing a beat, he grabs the poker and runs out the door, yelling at me to lock it. I wait in the dark, holding Hayden close. I don't know if it's to comfort him or because I need the comfort for myself. Together, we stand and shake, waiting for our hero to return.

After six knocks, Sean calls through the door that it's safe. I pause to assess the risk, then decide it's fine and let him in. As soon as the door is shut, he shakes his head and tells me nobody was there – that it was an after-effect of a bitter dream. I tell him Hayden saw it, too, and then Sean finally believes me. Only there's nothing he can do about it.

Because Ryan has vanished again.

Chapter 20
Then

WEEKS PASSED. *When the policemen came to tell me they no longer thought they could catch Ryan, I didn't know what to think. I stood there at my own front door, stunned at the idea of them leaving a killer out there in the big, wide world.*

I'd been doing so well, too – Hayden had been away for long enough that I was given a chance to think. I'd been spending my mornings taking long walks around the parks, stopping at cafés just for cups of herbal tea as my appetite hadn't come back yet. My mind was slowly being pieced back together, drawing me towards some semblance of sanity.

Then that progress was brought to a screeching halt.

There were two officers sent to deliver the news, but one waited by the lift. The other, Officer Edwards, delivered the news so informally. He was the only official I'd spoken to who had that personal touch – the others were so rigid and procedural, whereas this one spoke softly as his emerald eyes bored into me with great empathy.

'Are you going to be okay?' he asked. 'If there's anything I can do...'

'There's nothing. Thank you for bringing the news. It couldn't have been easy.'

'Compared to what you're going through, every-thing is easy. As long as you know we don't have any reason to think you and your son aren't safe. If we did, we'd have people watching the flat around the clock. But do call if you have any information.'

I nodded, thanked him, then shut the door and went to the balcony. I waited there, feeling like I was going to scream, throw up, or both. Adrenaline was pumping through my blood, leaving me unsure of what to do with myself. All I could do was wait until they left the building. When they got in their car, I threw some shoes and a coat on, then headed for the door.

It was the most desperate I'd ever been to leave the flat.

Those long morning walks started getting even longer, delaying the inevitable return to my home – which was now just the scene of Nick's murder. The more I stayed away, the less it felt like a bad place to be around. I was so lonely on my walking tours of London that it made me start to actually miss home. I missed Hayden, too. So badly that it hurt. We spoke on the phone every night, but that probably made it harder more than anything.

After another couple of weeks, I started to feel some version of my former self return. I was by the London Eye when it happened – like a switch had been flipped and my usual sulking mood turned into one of cherishment. It was obvious what had done it – Nick and I had been on the world's greatest Ferris wheel together, sipping champagne because he'd always wanted to do things in style. When we reached the top, the sunset had blinded me so hard that I spun around quickly, accidentally pouring my bubbly all over some poor man who proceeded to shout at us the entire time. It hadn't helped that Nick and I burst into hysterical laughter. The rest of the ride was so awkward that we'd never forget it.

That was the memory that changed everything for me.

I smiled and turned my back on the massive structure, holding the image so close to my heart. Until now, my selfishness had made me rely on Nick so much that I'd completely neglected my own son. It made me realise that – no matter how much I would miss my husband – there was a three-year-old boy wondering where his mum had gone. If I was ever going to be ready for a normal life again, this was it.

It was time to be with my family again.

ON A BEAUTIFUL SPRING MORNING, I stood at the main door of our building, staring up the street as the sunlight brushed its orangey-yellow hue against the tall buildings. Cars passed, the road buzzing with life as I waited to be reunited with my son. It didn't even matter that the cold was creeping between my clothes. All I wanted was Hayden.

Sure enough, my mother came around the corner with Hayden's backpack strapped to her shoulders, holding his hand as he tottered up the street. As soon as he saw me, his eyes lit up, and he tried to tear his hand free. When he realised he couldn't, he began to pull my mother towards me, *finally liberating himself as I knelt. He ran into my open arms so fast that it almost bowled me over. I hugged him tight, making the promise to myself in that moment that I would never leave him alone again.*

There was no reason he should lose both *parents.*

'It's good to see you,' my mother said flatly, like she didn't really mean it. When I picked Hayden up in my arms and stood, she looked me up and down. 'It's also good to see you've been looking after yourself. I've been worried sick.'

'Thank you for looking after him,' I said, ignoring the latter comment because it felt too insincere. 'I hope he wasn't any trouble. He's obviously been going through a hard time, so it wouldn't be a shock if he acted up.'

'No trouble at all. We had a great time together. Didn't we, Hayden?'

Hayden nodded violently, grinning again and then nuzzling into my neck. I'd never felt love quite like it – not even from Nick, which isn't to say that he and I didn't love each other more than life itself, but nothing on earth could compare to a mother's love.

Which made me question how my own mother really felt.

She handed me the bag and said goodbye, barely giving me a chance to thank her properly. As she turned to leave, I called to her and made her stop in her tracks. When she turned, I nodded towards the building's entrance.

'Do you want some brunch?' I asked.

A smile broke out on her face, as if it meant the world to her. It had occurred to me that she'd just been living with a family member for weeks, and then she had to return to her empty, lonely world. I was starting to see what that kind of life looked like, and I wouldn't have wished it on anyone. Least of all my mother, even if we never really did have a kinship.

She came upstairs, and we played together. Love and fun were returning to the flat, almost as if to cast colour on a black-and-white photo. Hayden played with the toys he hadn't seen in weeks, while my mother and I stayed in the kitchen, cooking up a storm. Her natural inclination was to micromanage and tell me I was doing everything wrong, so I appreciated it all the more when she bit her tongue and let me run the show.

After brunch, we all went for a family walk, taking Hayden to play in the park. I'd suddenly gone from having a broken family to a full and blossoming one. These were strange emotions for me because my mother had really been little more than a disciplinarian all my life. Now she smiled at me from the other side of the swing as we took it in turns pushing Hayden back and forth. The sun lit up her eyes, genuine happiness dwelling within them. I'll hold that image dear to me for the rest of my life – the only time I'd ever seen her truly happy.

When the time finally came to return home, I called her a cab. She stopped with one foot in the car door before making her way back to me. She hugged me truly and closely, like she really felt the affection I was also starting to feel.

'You take care,' she said. 'I love you.'

'I love you, too,' I said without hesitation.

She died that following week, on her sixty-eighth birthday. A heart attack, the doctors said. I should have been crushed, but I was just grateful that my final memory of her was one that would warm my heart in its coldest, darkest moments.

With any luck, she died feeling the same thing.

. . .

DAYS ROLLED INTO WEEKS, *weeks into months, and before I knew it, we were closing in on December. Some of the things I found hardest about being a widow – raising a child on my own, seeing happy couples holding hands as they strolled down the street – began to get a little easier. It's not like I wasn't sad any more, except I would no longer collapse with misery and depression. Even my front door was getting a little easier to look at. I no longer pictured Nick's lifeless body when I saw it. That's partly because I made the choice to buy a welcoming doormat that simply read:* Shrug off your burdens and put on a smile. You're home.

Cheesy, I know, but it worked.

Hayden was doing just as well, if not better, than I was. I'd been reintegrating him into some more toddler groups, letting him socialise and build friendships. It was amazing to see how fluent he was in body language, his open-armed demeanour drawing the other kids to him. So many of them laughed giddily whenever he tottered through the door. Hayden always ran to them as they did to him, meeting halfway and beginning their latest adventure in the soft play area. I was happy to sit back and watch him grow, learn, use his imagination.

Nick would have been so proud.

On one particular evening, namely the last day of November, Hayden broached the subject of his father. We were snuggled up in our living room, watching a Disney film and enjoying each other's company as a mother and son should. The film was about Rapunzel, though I forget the name of it, and the end showed the lost princess reunited with her parents.

I was really into it until he asked me.

'Where's my dad?'

Honestly, I didn't know what to tell him. But I knew that if I tiptoed around the issue for too long, then it would only become harder for him to come to terms with. He was four years old then, so I took the time to explain the concept of life and death, focusing more on the idea that Daddy's soul had returned to Heaven, which was where people became angels. He would be watching over his son for the rest of his life with a proud smile.

To be fair to Hayden, he took it really well. When he asked questions, I answered them. When he asked me what his father looked like, I felt my heart crumble at the idea that he was already forgetting Nick's face. I made a mental note to start *putting more photos of him around the flat – something I'd been avoiding for my own sanity.*

But my son's needs came first.

The film's credits came to an end, and Hayden was starting to fall asleep on me. I was relieved to have got away with the conversation, no tears involved for either of us. It was time to start thinking about sleep and how to get my son into his bed without waking him.

My phone chose an awful moment to ring.

The number was withheld, but I answered quickly just to silence the ringtone.

'Hello?' I whispered, wincing as Hayden stirred.

'Hello, Kate.'

I knew the voice immediately. If not for the cruel, taunting tone, then for the shudder that rippled through my body. My skin grew goose-bumps, and I looked to the window to see if it was open. It wasn't. The voice was what caused my sudden chill.

Ryan's voice.

'Just so you know, I'll be seeing you.'

That was all he said before he hung up. My phone was still pressed to my ear, rattling in my shaking hand as I was instantly drawn back to the worst moment of my life – the night Nick was taken from me and a man – Ryan, surely – had fled the scene. The horrors of my discovery repeated again, nipping away at me like a thousand piranha hell-bent on making me bleed.

Since then, all I've ever felt is fear.

Chapter 21
Now

AFTER A RESTLESS NIGHT of all huddling together in the living room, I'm up and walking around at the crack of dawn. Hayden is still dozing peacefully, and I'm dying to make a coffee, but Sean reminds me it'll disturb the poor kid's sleep.

Things are already hard enough.

Lowering our voices to a whisper, we gather at the far end of the kitchen. Sean holds me close, rubbing my back to soothe me as he clearly sees how anxious I am. Despite knowing that Ryan was nearby, none of us expected to actually see him, least of all by the window in the middle of the night. It was a shock to the system that pushed me over the edge.

Now I have to explain my desperation.

'I don't want to stay here,' I say into Sean's chest.

'We've been over this. There's nothing we can do.'

'Not unless *you* go.'

Sean's chest rises and falls with the weight of a heavy sigh. 'If you want me to try making it through the forest, I'll do it with no questions asked. But it's important that you're sure about this. Once I start the trek, there's no going back.'

Although my heart is set on it, I do give it one last thought. I'd be exposing myself to Ryan, but the odds of surviving up here another few days aren't looking too great. It sounds like a stupid thing to do, but really, we have no choice.

'You should go.'

Sean doesn't argue as he lets go of me and kisses me on the head. The next thing I know, he's wrapping up warm and sliding his feet into the hiking boots he'd been smart enough to bring with him. When I'm done nibbling on my fingernails, I head to the coat stand and take a waterproof coat, helping him into it by the door.

'For the record, I don't like this,' he whispers.

'Neither do I, but it's better than getting murdered in our sleep.'

Sean huffs and glances out the nearby window. Then his eyes widen as if he has an idea – a light bulb moment that excites me more than it should, opening myself up to inevitable disappointment. He tells me he'll be right back, letting in an icy gust of wind as he goes outside. I watch from the window while he heads next door. He and Frank talk for some time. All I can hear is a slight mumble and Hayden's heavy breathing from behind me. I can't help but wonder what the bright idea is, but I'm starting to figure it out.

When he gets back, Sean takes my hand and tells me Frank is going to look out for me. Apparently, he offered to go with Sean in case there was some kind of accident in the slippery mud, but Sean insisted that he stay here to look out for me.

It should make me feel safer, but it doesn't.

Nothing can.

'Don't forget your phone,' I tell Sean, hugging him closely and praying he has a safe journey through the trees. 'How long do you think it should take?'

'Hours,' he says. 'Even when I get to Malcolm's house, we'll still have to come up here. It's getting dark early, so maybe he won't even want to drive in the dark. I'd say maybe I should leave at night so he could drive up in the day, but then I might not even make it.'

'Are you sure this is safe?'

'Like you said, safer than the alternative.'

'I'm worried about you.'

'Don't be. If all goes well, I should be back with the jeep before dark.'

It feels too good to be true, and maybe it is. The mental image of the jeep arriving to carry us to safety is so exciting that I don't know what to do with myself. I settle for a long, hard kiss with Sean before he heads out the door with everything he needs to get us help. Long after he disappears between the trees, I stand there watching in the silence as the wind lashes at my face, throwing my hair all over the place.

It's eerily quiet up here. It always was, but now that I know Hayden and I are alone, I'm suddenly haunted by just how isolated we are. Sure, Frank and Jeanie are watching over us, but will that be enough if Ryan decides to come back? We're miles from civilisation and completely helpless – two old folks, a petite widow, and a kid.

Somehow, I don't like our odds.

. . .

NIGHT FALLS, and Sean still hasn't returned.

I know it's pointless, but I keep checking on my phone as if I'll suddenly gain a signal and be able to make a call. I know I'm the one who wanted to be alone in the middle of nowhere, but now it's become my biggest mistake. Because it's not just me and my son at risk.

If anything happens to Sean out there, I'll never forgive myself.

We've put all the lights on dim and closed all the curtains. This way, Ryan won't have any way of knowing which room we're in or, therefore, which window he should break into if he decides to do so. The thought of it alone makes my skin crawl.

I keep Hayden close to me all night. He does talk about protecting me if and when the time comes, which is super cute, but I want him to know he has nothing to fear. I explain to him that Frank and Jeanie will help us if we get desperate. Even if they don't see Ryan enter the cottage, at least we can make a run for it and bang on their door. They even said it themselves – they're there if we need them.

It does make me feel a bit safer, but not much. The clock is ticking, and with every passing minute, I can't help thinking something has happened to Sean. The wind has picked up, a light drizzle hammering against the windows in the dead of night. But there's a groaning sound, as though the trees are yawning in the wind, their stretched branches reaching out to consume us. It's a bitter reminder that this forest might be our final resting place.

As the evening goes by, Hayden tells me how tired he is and that he wants to go to bed. I'm not sure it's a good idea to go alone, so I go with him and let him fall asleep in my arms as if he's still that confused four-year-old, wishing his daddy was here.

But it's all right.

Mummy is here.

And help is on its way.

It's hard to say exactly when I fell asleep, but I wake up and check my watch. The wind is stronger than ever, the trees still creaking under the gale's pressure. It's a little after nine. The night is relatively young, but there's still no sign of Sean. I dread to think what happened to him, but I'll remain optimistic. What other choice do I have?

I've also been fighting the urge to pee for too long, so I creep out of bed and make my way to the bathroom. I keep the lights off while I do my business because I don't want to encourage an unwelcome visitor by announcing my whereabouts. I finish up, ignore the flush so it can't be heard from outside, then wash my hands.

The moment I step out of the bathroom, I stop dead.

There's movement at the kitchen window. This would be enough to creep me out already, but the movement is coming from *inside*. In the dim glow of the oven's overhead light, I see the figure creeping in, setting foot on the sink. I don't know how he got in without breaking the glass, but he's stepping down from the worktop with a knife glinting under the soft light.

I'm in a trance, but I must break free. Even though it feels like spiders are scurrying all over my skin, the hairs standing up all over my body, I know it's time to move – to sneak back into the bedroom and get Hayden.

Before Ryan gets there first.

It's too late.

Ryan enters the living room and glances down the hall. I don't know if the shadows are helping conceal me, but he stands there to assess the situation for a moment before turning around. My heart is thumping the whole time while I stand frozen.

The moment his back is turned, I do the only thing I can.

I hide.

The towel cupboard is the nearest door to me, so I twist the knob quickly and quietly, tiptoe inside, then pull the door shut in front of me. It's pitch-black in here, blinding me completely while I hold my breath and pray he doesn't come this way.

Then the footsteps begin again.

They're growing louder, coming towards me step by careful step. The floorboards creak under his weight. All I see in my mind's eye is that knife in his hand. Is it the same knife that killed my husband? Is that what he'll use to finish me? Will he then go for—

Hayden!

God, if anything happens to my son, then I'll never forgive myself. But rushing out now would be suicide, so all I can do is listen carefully to the heavy footfalls and hope he goes into the main bedroom first. If I could just be lucky enough for that to happen, I can rush into Hayden's room and lock the door. Better yet, Hayden could already have woken up and taken his escape through the window. Wouldn't that be something?

'I know you're in here somewhere, Kate.'

It's definitely Ryan's voice, without a shadow of a doubt. I guess this – coupled with the face I saw in the window – proves beyond all measure that he was the one who killed Nick. My hate for him rages out of control, only rivalled by my icy terror.

'Don't even think about jumping out at me,' he says snidely. 'If you do, you'll regret it. Show me where you're hiding, and I'll make your death nice and quick. There's no reason for this to get ugly, eh?'

The little chortle he gives next rattles my bones. I just know he's ready to kill – it's not his first time, and it probably won't be his last. But I have to get out of here sooner or later. If he finds me first, there will be nobody to protect Hayden. If he gets to Hayden first, he could easily apply some pressure to find my whereabouts.

The only way to win is to beat him there.

I wait for the footsteps to pass. There's silence then. My hand won't stay still as it reaches for the doorknob, which I twist before slowly opening the door. My breath caught in my now full lungs, I poke my head out and take a little look around, praying the old wood doesn't creak with any of my small, terrified little movements.

Then I see him.

Ryan has his back to me, standing still between the main bedroom and Hayden's room. Both doors are shut, and it looks as if he's contemplating which one to try first. I'm frozen on the spot, praying he takes the main bedroom so I can make a run for my son. I even think about smashing something over his head, but Ryan always was far stronger than me.

Finally, he moves left.

Into the main bedroom.

This is it, I tell myself. My one and only chance to reach Hayden's room and lock the killer out. I wait a couple of seconds for him to head deeper into the bedroom, then begin my steady creep along the hallway, holding my breath the whole time.

That's when the floorboard whines under my foot.

I freeze for a split second, every possible eventuality playing out in my mind. In that same fraction of a moment, my senses rush back to me, and I know what to do.

Without wasting a single second, I make a dash

for the bedroom. Ryan must have heard it because he's laughing like a maniac as his footsteps pound closer to me from the other room. I'm sick with fear as I run into Hayden's room, reaching for the door. I miss in the dark. I try again, this time finding purchase as Ryan comes lunging at me. Desperate to keep my family safe, I slam it shut and turn the key just as Ryan's full weight crashes against the wood.

'Open it now, Kate! You can't get away from me!'

Hayden jolts out of his sleep then, rushes out of bed, and helps me lean against the door, supporting the frame as his father's killer does everything in his power to break it down – to enter the room and put us down for good.

Chapter 22
Sean

SEAN COMES to in a deep pool of ice-cold mud. It's barely moist any more as the wintery weather has frozen it around him. His muscles ache from tensing in the extreme conditions, but he forces himself to his feet because that's what he promised to do.

How long has he been out, he wonders? It could be minutes or hours, but the sunlight was still visible through the break in the trees when he slid. He thinks back to that moment with humiliation and a deep sense of failure; first, he avoided the dangerously close flutter of birds buzzing past his face, and then his sleeve caught on a branch. As he turned to wriggle free, he lost his footing. That's the last thing he remembers, although he'd rather not.

Doing his best to ignore the searing pain in the back of his head – and the dryness of his tongue as he shivers uncontrollably – he clambers to his feet and presses on through Deepwood Forest. His ankle burns with raw agony, probably twisted during the fall. Another thing to be ashamed of because he should have got back to Kate and the kid already.

Five minutes pass, and Sean begins to wonder if he can make it at all. He hears Malcolm's voice in his head, mocking him for his foolish effort. He was warned not to try coming through the forest, most of all in the night when some were said to have never returned.

Is that because of the trek or because Ryan makes a habit of murder up here?

It doesn't matter now. All that matters is that he makes it down the bank and through the thick, scratching branches that claw at his now bare arms. It might be the forest that kills him, or it might be the cold setting in, but he's determined to do one last thing before he dies.

He has to get help for the others.

As he passes down a steep incline, desperately

holding onto the trees for support, some branches snap behind him. Not the usual sort, rustling in the violent winds like they have been this whole time, but a full, weighty snap. He stops to look behind him. There's movement in the black, but that could be anything. The night's darkness offers no comfort.

But he must press on. It's been hours since he left Kate alone with Hayden up there, and he doesn't like to think about what might happen to them. Hell, it could have *already* happened to them, and – as much as he hates to admit it – there's no denying it's mostly his fault.

The branches behind him snap again. Sean panics and, just in case he's being followed, doubles his pace. He bites through the pain in his ankle, his muscles, the skin on his hands tearing apart in the freezing temperatures. It's all he can do to stay upright because, far below, he can see the light of Malcolm's house, a beacon in the dead of night. If he can have just one last thing in his life, it's to get there in time for Kate.

Otherwise, he wouldn't know what to do.

Chapter 23
Then

IT WOULD BE *an understatement to say I was surprised when the leading detective arrived at my door. Until then, I'd been under the impression that he was simply following procedure and doing the things he simply had to do because the job demanded it. I'd never had so much as a hint that he cared about Nick's murder any more than he did for other homicides. Which was fair, I supposed, because Nick was only special for those who knew him.*

'Mrs. Bailey,' he said curtly at my doorstep. 'May I speak with you?'

Needless to say, I opened my door wider for him to come in. It'd been two days since receiving the threatening call from Ryan, and it was only now being addressed. I wondered what it might take for the detective to put some real effort in. I was, of course, aware that maybe I was being unfair. It wasn't easy to find one man on the whole planet. That stuff was reserved for the films and TV shows. Works of fiction.

The detective – whose name I couldn't place – let himself in, his wide shoulders taking up a large portion of the entranceway. I offered him a seat, but he said it wouldn't take long and that he'd be out of my hair soon enough. I wasn't sure what to make of that because, if anything, I wanted him in my hair more than ever.

Whatever it took to find Ryan.

'Didn't you have a kid with you?' he asked. 'A young boy?'

'My son, yes. He's at playschool.'

'Ah.' He stroked his grey stubble, an audible scratching sound filling the silence. 'I found a note on my desk saying you've had an interaction with Ryan Wyatt. Would you care to fill me in on the details?'

So I told him. The exact time that I had memorised, the unknown number he'd called from, and the precise words he'd used to threaten me with. The detective listened with great interest, taking notes on a small pad from his breast pocket. There was no judgement in his face – not so much as a little suspicion or surprise – but he did clap his notepad shut.

'Do you feel like your life might be in danger?' he asked.

I shrugged. 'To a degree. I spoke with the owner of the building, and we're having a password panel put into the lift. After that's installed, nobody will be able to reach this floor without my unique code, which I'll be changing regularly just to be safe.'

'That sounds very sensible. What about your son?'

'Do you think Ryan would do something to an innocent kid?'

'I wouldn't like to say one way or the other, but if you feel like it's a possibility, then we can have someone watch out for you. It won't be full-time, but a little extra protection might be enough to warn off someone who's thinking of doing something drastic.'

'How long could they stay?'

'Working shifts?' He bit his lip. 'Maybe three or four days per week. More, if there's another interaction between the two of you. But this needs to escalate in order for us to use resources on it. Until then, this is the best we can do.'

I thought long and hard about what to do next, then eventually decided on leaving it as is. If something else happened, then I'd gladly welcome an officer to watch over us. Maybe Officer Edwards, the kind one with the caring green eyes.

'Very well,' the detective said. 'But you could also consider moving.'

'I can't do that,' I explained. 'This is our home.'

'I'm just saying, a change of scenery and perhaps your name might make it a lot harder for this Ryan fella to find you. If I were you and wanted to take extra measures, those are the ones I'd take. Goodbye, Mrs. Bailey.'

After seeing him out, I lingered in the lonely hallway, gazing down at the spot where Nick was killed. It seems awfully morbid, but I didn't want to get away from that reminder. Even if it did make my stomach churn every time I saw the small patch of marble, I had to remember this was the home we'd bought together. Sure, it was mostly his money – which is to say it was almost completely on him – but we'd selected it together. We'd picked out the furniture as a joint decision. Everything around me was a gentle reminder of the relationship I had to my husband, my best friend, and the love of my life.

There was no way I was moving.

Even if my life was in danger.

'JUST SO YOU KNOW, *I'll be seeing you.*'

That was what Ryan had said, and it'd been lodged in my head ever since, like shrapnel from some explosive blast. The longer it was in there, the more damage it was doing. I was already starting to question everyone and everything around me, so what might happen when my terror and paranoia started to reach new heights?

I knew something bad was about to happen every time I looked out my window. The street I lived on was plagued with lights, the windows up the street caked in spray-on snow. People were singing and cheering merrily, those bloody festive tunes making their annual resurgence once again. Even the weather was joining in this time, with sleet raining heavily against the glass, pretending to be real snow.

It was Christmastime, and I hated every second of it.

Hayden didn't seem to mind, since his memory of Nick was fading. It pained me to think that he only vaguely recalled that a man used to live with us and that he loved us both so madly. Before long, he would probably forget entirely, and then he would start to ask questions about what his father was like. And I would tell him – that he was the sweetest, most genuine person I'd ever had the great honour of knowing.

I wouldn't mention that his best friend had killed him in our home.

At least the photos I'd put up were becoming a part of the furniture. They were everywhere: on all the shelves, lined up on top of the TV unit. I was in some of those pictures, grinning like an idiot because I'd had no idea what was coming. Hayden was in all but one, nuzzling into his father's neck like they were going to be best friends for life.

It made me sick to look at them, but he needed to know.

We'd done away with the Christmas tree that year. There were no decorations in our home, but I wasn't cruel enough to deprive my son of presents. I had some stuff ready for him, except he would wake up on the big day to find them at the bottom of his bed, seeing as there was no tree to place them under. Some might think it was a selfish move on my part, but it was the first Christmas without my husband, and everywhere I looked, there was an obscenely big reminder of how happy everyone was supposed to be. It was a time for families, they all said, and ours had been taken from us. Even my mother was gone this year.

Still, I made the most of it for Hayden's sake. He spent the day opening presents with wide-eyed wonder, giggling with excitement as he frantically tore open the wrapping and exclaiming thrilled gratitude at what he'd uncovered. It wasn't all bad, I saw in that moment – if I could simply protect my son from the horrors of this season, I was doing something right.

It was me who had the rough ride.

Because I couldn't stop thinking about Ryan.

What exactly had he meant by saying he'd be seeing me? Was he planning another homicide, exacting his revenge for reporting him to the police? Did he still intend to claim the intercourse he'd so desperately wanted? Whatever he was up to, I had to stay vigilant, so the security in my flat was stepped up a notch with shrill alarms and extra locks. Even the lift had been fortified with a password that only I knew.

Nobody was going to get to me.

Much less my son.

. . .

New Year wasn't so bad. Again, it was the first one as a broken family, but it distracted all of London from the insufferable day that had landed only one week prior. The decorations were still up, but they wouldn't last long. For many, it was the last day of keeping them up.

This may be bold, but I didn't hate the idea of celebrating a fresh start. Hayden had been harping on and on about seeing the fireworks, and I didn't want to deny him. In fact, it would probably do us both some good to get out of the flat for a while. With that, I dressed us both up nice and warm, then took him down to the riverside by Westminster for the viewing.

It didn't seem to matter that we could have seen them from our window.

The Underground was packed out, all of us cramming together like sardines in a tin. I kept Hayden close to me, not once letting go of his hand because I couldn't stand to lose another loved one. Crowds had never been a problem for me, but I seemed to see Ryan's face everywhere – on every passenger who entered the train, closing in on us before the doors whirred shut. We were trapped. I was sweating.

By the time we got out, we'd finished the walk to

the riverside by following the masses of people. London had completely transformed due to the firework display that was due to light up the sky soon enough. There were people everywhere, a lot of the roads closed off and new routes being created. It was hard to get around without people nudging into me, their own selfish urgency to find a good standing spot trumping their manners. I was doing all I could to protect Hayden, but when a heavy thud sent me sprawling onto the ground, my instincts told me to let go or bring him down with me.

Pain exploded in my knee and up my leg. My wrists took a lot of the fall, hitting the concrete with a shocking thud. I didn't care that it was wet and dirty because I was instantly back on my feet, my arms feeling like they were on fire as I scanned for Hayden in the crowd.

But he was gone.

'Hayden!' I yelled at the top of my lungs, shoving people aside and passing through crowds. I felt weightless with anxiety as I continued to call his name, begging people to tell me, 'Have you seen a boy? He's four. I can't find my son!'

A crowd of over thirty hooligans were chanting as they came around the corner, so nobody could hear me any longer. I'd never felt more like a failure as a parent than I did at that moment. My knees were weak with horror, but I ran around none-theless, hell-bent on getting my son back safely into my arms.

I found him on the pavement with his back to the wall. He was crying, rubbing his red face. I ran to him, still pushing people out of my way as I saw how small and fragile he looked – a tiny boy in a massive city. When I reached him, I scooped him into my arms and let him cry into my chest. I hugged him so fiercely, swearing to never let him go.

'I lost you, Mummy.'

'I know, sweetheart. Mummy fell.'

We didn't get to see the fireworks that night. Not from the riverbank anyway. We headed straight home, got some tasty snacks out, and watched from our penthouse flat. I hated that I couldn't perform such a simple task as taking him to see fireworks, but as I ran the situation through my head that night, I realised I'd been worried about something in particular.

During my search, I'd thought maybe Ryan had got to him.

Chapter 24

Now

RYAN STOPS thumping against the door, leaving Hayden and me to stare at each other with the same terrified, questioning expression. We're each soaked through with sweat, silent in the dimly lit room, undoubtedly wondering the same thing.

Is he gone?

At least the banging has stopped. I haven't heard footsteps, so it's likely he could still be there. I point towards the window and whisper to Hayden that it's our way out of this mess. I don't know where we would go when we're out, but next door seems like a safe bet. As long as we can actually get inside without Ryan grabbing us.

We ease away from the door and creep across

the room. I unlatch the window slowly and care-fully, wincing at the rusty squeak of the lock. When it's fully open, I think it's easier for me to climb through first – if not to help my son through, then to check that Ryan isn't out there waiting for us, leaving the door because he's figured out our plan.

It seems clear, though it's hard to see when the night is this dark. I take a final glance back at the door, confirm this is the best course of action, then take a breath. My nerves are shot, the adrenaline making it feel like my blood is on fire, but I must persevere.

I begin my climb through the window, but that's as far as I get. A pair of hands shoot through. A furious scream emits from the attacker's mouth. Hayden and I step back, both screaming as I barely escape Ryan's grip. But he begins to climb through the window, his limbs working like a scurrying insect. My back is slick with cold sweat.

'Run!' I tell Hayden.

We both move fast, but it doesn't feel fast enough. As I close the bedroom door behind us, I see Ryan has gone. The window is now free, but that may be some trick. Hayden makes a break for the front door, but I hiss at him to stop because I've discovered a new horror.

Ryan could be outside any one of these walls.

It's not the best thing we can do, but we have to hide. If we can just stay still long enough, he might get fed up and enter the cottage once more. Although that puts us more in harm's way, at least we'd know exactly where he is.

That's better than nothing.

I lead by example, hiding behind the floor-length curtains in the living room. If Ryan passes this window now, we're as good as dead. But where else could we hide? Under the bed is too far from the front door, and anywhere else is too obvious. So we stand there side by side, our shaking bodies ruffling the fabric ever so slightly. I pull Hayden closer to the window, doing my best to conceal us from our hunter.

Then the door opens.

'You might as well give up,' Ryan says. 'You're not getting out of here. Even if you did, where would you go? To the neighbours? They can't help you any more than your boyfriend can, and we both know what happens to men you rely on.'

I know what he's doing, but it's not going to

work. He wants me to lose my temper and come out, or maybe just sob like a helpless coward and give away our position. I won't give him the satisfaction, so I hold my son's hand and listen closely as the footsteps move towards the far end of the living room, stopping once more.

'Kate, Kate, Kate,' he says so calmly it's creepy. 'Why make it so hard?'

I won't answer. I'm not that stupid. In fact, I'm smart enough to know he hasn't found us and probably won't unless he has a lot more time. That's something I don't intend to give him because as soon as he heads down the hallway, it's time to make a break for it.

It's now or never.

My heart leaps into my throat as I rip back the curtain. Grabbing Hayden's hand, I sprint for the door. Ryan hears the footsteps, turns, and chases us like a lion charging through a herd of gazelles. I don't look back, nor do I stop to shut the door behind me.

All I do is run.

We make it outside into the dark, where the freezing wind violently assaults us. Hayden yelps at the sudden drop in temperature, and even my own breath is taken away. But it can't stop us – *won't* stop us – as we desperately rush to Frank and Jeanie's cottage. Only they can help us now, and if they don't get to the door fast enough, then only one thing can happen.

Ryan will kill us in seconds.

I'M HITTING the door so hard that I'm practically punching it. Meanwhile, my intense gaze is set on the corner of our own cottage, where Ryan stumbles out and looks around. Hayden hugs me, squeezing so hard because he knows what's about to happen.

'Open up!' I scream at the top of my lungs. 'Help!'

By now, Ryan is running, darting towards us at an ungodly speed. I hit the door harder, faster, more frantically as the wind pulls at my hand, lashing my hair all over the place. Ryan is still coming. There's no answer on the door. We can't run because the mud is too thick. We can't fight because Ryan has a knife that's bigger than my forearm.

This is the end – I just know it – but it doesn't stop me from beating the door with the heel of my hand. Kicking it. Screaming. Praying for this one last miracle because it's the only thing that will save us, yet Ryan is so close, closer still, raising the knife high above his head.

We fall through the door as it opens. Ryan's deadly slash misses me by an inch. I scramble to my feet, haul Hayden up to his, then slam the door behind me. Jeanie stands there, stunned and helpless, and I slide the bolt across. Ryan thumps against the thick wood, screaming like an enraged animal because he just missed his prey.

But we're only safe for the time being.

THE HITTING on the door stops. I stand there with Hayden behind me, protecting him at all costs. Jeanie is at my side, and all three of us are staring like something bad will inevitably happen. And it will – if Ryan doesn't leave, then we're all in trouble.

'Was... that him?' Jeanie asks, her voice sounding frail with the new quiver.

'That was him,' I confirm, trying to keep my own voice steady because I have to stay strong. If I can't convince myself that I can handle this situa-

tion, I might as well walk out there and get myself
killed right now.

I look around the inside of the cottage, chilled
by the uncomfortable silence. It's a similar floor
plan to the one we'd won a magical week-long trip
in, only this one is more spacious. The furniture is
more worn, the paintings on the walls and the
photos dotted around making it feel more like a
home and less like a winter getaway. My attention
then turns to the windows, making sure all the
curtains are shut so we can't be watched by the
killer creep outside.

It's only then that I notice a certain absence.

'Where's Frank?' I ask.

Jeanie has a hand on her neck, tucking herself
up tight. Her wide, frightened eyes haven't left the
door, and they don't until she slowly blinks away
from it and finds herself back in the present
moment. 'He was worried about Sean, so he
dressed up warm and went after him.'

'Into the forest? It's dangerous out there.'

'It's dangerous in *here*.'

She has a point, and I do appreciate that
someone is looking out for Sean. The only down-
side is that now we're alone in this small building

with nobody to protect us. Until now, I've been relying on Sean and Frank to keep us safe.

It looks like that plan is out the window.

'Mum, I'm scared,' Hayden says.

I'm scared, too, but I won't tell him as much. I look to Jeanie for guidance because I don't want to treat her home like a fallout shelter, helping ourselves to anything we might need or acting like it's our very own refuge.

She doesn't take long to come around, asking if any of us are hurt and then seeing to it that Hayden is distracted by kneeling in front of him and holding his hand. 'You look a little on the cold side, dear. Maybe you'd like some hot chocolate to warm you up?'

Hayden glares up at me, and I fake a smile, then nod.

'Yes, please,' he says.

'And you, Kate?'

'I'm okay, thanks.'

Jeanie heads to the open-plan kitchen and sets to making a single cup of hot chocolate. To tell the truth, I'm far too rattled to think about putting anything in my body. I'm sweating, shaking, and need a moment to recover where my son can't see me. The last thing I want is for my fear and discomfort to influence how he's feeling. Despite just being chased by a knife-wielding maniac, we need to find a way to stay calm and collected. Besides, Ryan seems to have given up and walked away.

For now.

I take Hayden to the living room and sit with him. He falls into the large cushion. I take a seat by his side. He's still shaking – we both are, which is to be expected. And in the silence that's only disturbed by the boiling of an electric kettle, I begin to wonder just how Sean and Frank are getting along. Have they made it to Malcolm's yet?

Are they on their way back to save us?

Jeanie comes in within a couple of minutes, planting a mug of hot chocolate on the coffee table in front of Hayden. He thanks her, the sprinkles and marshmallows distracting him as they were intended to do. She warns him that it's still piping hot, and I mouth a thank you to her while she takes a seat in the armchair across from us.

'Should I be worried?' she asks. 'Will he come in here?'

'It's hard to say because he did break into our place, but this seems slightly more fortified.' I look to the door that's way thicker than ours. The walls seem reinforced, the windows double-glazed. These are mere guesses based on the fact I can't hear a single breath of wind. Not even creaking wood from the patio outside. 'I don't think he'll get in.'

'If he does, you should just run. It's probably your only hope.'

'What about you?'

'I'm too old to go leaping through a forest on a winter's night.'

I don't like the way she's speaking, as if she's willing to sacrifice herself for us. It's especially unsuitable because Hayden is hearing every word. No child should have to endure half the stuff he's gone through tonight.

At the thought of keeping up appearances, I ask Jeanie if she wouldn't mind watching him for a minute while I go to freshen up. She tells me it's fine, directing me to the bathroom that – unsurprisingly – is in the same layout ours is.

When I'm alone, I stare at my messy reflection in the mirror above the sink. My mousy-brown hair is coated to my forehead with sweat, the frayed ends looking like a mess of spiders' legs spread across my face. There are dark hollows under my eyes, but I take care of it all with some splashing of warm water and a comb I find on the shelf. I wash out the latter when I'm done, linger long enough for my hands to stop trembling, then decide it's safe for my son to see me. I do want to maintain the vibe of a calm ocean, after all.

Feeling like I've done enough, I exit the bathroom and make my way back to the living room. But something stops me, stealing my attention. The hallway is plastered in hanging photos, with Frank and Jeanie seeming to age as the wall goes on. I stop long enough to admire them, as if watching their entire lives in a single line. They seem to have met young, maybe in the fifties, judging by their hairstyles. They grew older in each collection of frames, continuing until they're in a professionally taken shot, holding their newborn baby. I smile at the sentiment because I've been there myself, and it's a magical feeling.

But then a dark cloud draws over me.

That baby seems to be growing into a kid pretty fast, then a teenager with a slightly recognisable face. A metre or so along the wall, that face moulds into something more familiar, taking shape as the same face that's haunted my dreams for many years. My shakes come back, a sudden bout of terror seizing me as I slowly put two and two together.

Then I realise with a streak of unrivalled horror that I know their son.

His name is Ryan Wyatt.

Chapter 25
Then

MARCH CAME AROUND *before I knew it. This freaked me out a surprising amount because the first day of January had felt like a reset button for my emotions. I'd been doing so well for those first couple of months, bonding with Hayden and starting to feel safe. Ryan hadn't even crossed my mind in weeks – his phone call was starting to look like mere tough talk.*

At least I was coming to terms with what had happened to Nick. That wasn't to say I'd forgotten him and didn't wish every day that he would miraculously spring back to life, but I was starting to accept that things were... well, what they were. My independence was coming back, and I smiled from time to time.

If that wasn't progress, what was?

On a beautiful spring morning, I took the long walk to my nearest supermarket after dropping Hayden off at playschool. This was starting to become the time of day when I'd train myself to be happy, appreciating the finer things in life like a sunny day or the sounds of a busy city as its citizens went about their daily lives. Even chores like shopping felt like bliss because I could just be myself and not have to worry about being a mum.

I was standing in the middle of a shopping aisle when my life changed again.

'Kate?' came a man's voice from behind me. It was deep but somehow soft. Familiar, but I couldn't quite figure out how without turning around to see the green-eyed officer beaming at me. 'You're Kate Bailey, aren't you?'

'Indeed I am,' I said, nodding politely. 'You're that cop, aren't you?'

'Yeah, that's me.' His smile broadened. 'I'm surprised you remember me.'

Before I could get the words out, I disgusted myself by thinking of exclaiming that I couldn't possibly forget him. I wasn't fooling myself – he was easy on the eye – but my stomach churned at the thought of betraying Nick like that. Long gone or not, he was still the love of my life. Being with someone else just felt wrong.

'Sorry if I made you uncomfortable. I just... how are you?'

'I'm...'

'That's a stupid question.'

I laughed, which made him laugh, too.

'It really is a stupid question. But you know, the answer isn't as simple as you'd think. It's taking time, but we're getting there.'

'We,' he mused. 'Oh, you have that boy, right? Aiden, is it?'

'Hayden.'

'That's right. Sorry.'

The aisle suddenly became awkward and quiet. I could hear the sounds of the cashier beeping in the distance, some shopping trollies rattling around outside, but other than that, it felt like we were frozen in time. I unlocked my eyes from the officer's, looking down at the two different kinds of jam I had in each hand.

'I'd better—'

'Yeah.'

'So, uh...'

'Yeah.'

He made a move as if to go, then pointed at the

jams. 'By the way, that's Hartley's. The raspberry is amazing, but don't even think about the apricot. It tastes like glue, and the consistency is no better.'

I laughed at the meaningless attempt to continue the conversation, but it was oddly endearing. I appreciated that he remembered me and that he'd taken the time to stop and have a conversation with me. I also didn't want to sound rude, so I opened the chat back up.

'I didn't catch your name,' I told him. 'Was it... Edwards?'

'Good memory. Officer Edwards, or just Sean if you prefer.'

'Well, Sean, how is the strawberry jam?'

'The best.' He mimed a chef's kiss, and I giggled.

God, I felt like a silly little girl with a crush. Once more, I experienced shame and disgust for the way I was feeling, having to tell myself that it was perfectly normal to find a man attractive. Especially when he was as nice as Sean was.

'Would you maybe like to go grab a drink?' he asked.

'Ah.' I froze. 'I don't know. It's the middle of the morning.'

'Yeah. The drink in question is coffee.'

'Oh. Um... I don't know.'

'That's fine,' he said. 'I understand you might be feeling a little bad on your husband, but it's entirely innocent. I promise you. One coffee, that's all.'

It felt like a fork in the road for my entire life. I knew how dangerous a single coffee could be when you're enjoying it with good conversation from a handsome man. But I also felt like I was entitled to live a little – as though I would never truly heal until I started treating myself to the simplest things, like a hot drink on a cold morning.

'Just one coffee?' I confirmed.

'Just one. And maybe a muffin.'

Finally, I nodded. 'All right, let's do it.'

I WOULD BE LYING if I said we didn't get on like a house on fire.

As it turned out, we both loved films, long walks, and were quite 'indoorsy' people. Our perfect idea of a Friday night was snuggled up on the sofa with a loved one and watching a horror film, followed by a comedy for good balance. That was what we sort of arranged, but I didn't know at the time if it was a hypothetical suggestion.

Best to assume it was.

The more we talked, indulging in one caramel latte more than initially planned, the more we discovered things we liked about the other. My worries about betraying Nick seemed to slowly melt away. Perhaps it was because my heart was slowly being set on another, but it also helped that Sean had the decency to ask about Nick.

As soon as the words left his mouth, I froze.

'Sorry,' I said, stumbling for words. 'Could you repeat that?'

'I asked what Nick was like as a person.'

'Oh. Well, he...' How do you describe the best person you've ever known to basically a stranger? With honesty, that's how. 'Not once did he put himself first. He was very warm and generous. Liked to help people in any way he could. But not in one of those passion project sorts of ways – people were never just subjects to him. He genuinely cared for his fellow man, doing a lot of charity work wherever he could.

'Before we moved into the flat, we lived in a houseshare with a woman who had kids. Even though he was working a ridiculous number of hours at the surgery, he'd make sure my needs were met and then spent every waking moment building a tree house in the back garden. Obviously, he used

his own supplies, spending his own money on the materials.'

Sean smirked from one side of his mouth. 'Sounds like a big project.'

'It was. The kids loved it. And he didn't even accept their gratitude. All he wanted was for them to promise they would never stop using their imaginations in the hope that, someday, they could grow up to build something for other children. That was Nick in a nutshell.'

It didn't even strike me as strange when Sean reached across the table and rested his hand on mine. I didn't pull away because my mind was so deep in one of the many fond memories of Nick that nothing could turn my mood around. If anything, it helped with the illusion that Nick was still here in some way.

Because Sean's touch felt like his.

'Listen,' he said after a comfortable silence, using a napkin to mop up crumbs from the table and scoop them onto the plate, which he pushed aside. 'I want to invite you out for dinner, and if you don't feel like you're able to move past your husband, then I completely understand. I'd just like to say ahead of time that I won't rush you into anything. It's dinner with a dating connotation, but *entirely at your speed. If you're not ready, that's absolutely fine. I can either be your friend or stay as far away as you'd like me to.'*

I was blown away by his directness, but I always was drawn to a man who got to the point. Besides, it'd been long enough that I deserved a friend at the very least, so if it truly was going to be at the speed I chose, then I had nothing to fear.

That's why I agreed to dinner.

Dinner went so well – *Sean took me to a beautiful but quiet Italian place where we ate by the window. Normally I'd hate something like that, feeling like a goldfish in a bowl, but I was so swept up by the budding romance that I didn't much care.*

Like the true gentleman he'd appeared to be, he then walked me home and didn't so much as attempt a kiss on the cheek. I really appreciated that he was keeping things slow, being patient with me while I continued to mourn another man. Not many people would put up with a widow who still harped on about her dead husband, but I was still very much in love with Nick. I always would be, until the day I died.

If he couldn't accept that, we were just wasting time.

I didn't see him for three or four weeks after that because he was only free in the evenings, and I didn't want to leave Hayden with a babysitter just yet. As much as I wanted to have my own life, I was still mildly aware that Ryan was still out there. And whether he'd truly been the one that killed Nick or not, he'd still threatened to see me soon.

It was funny how time went by, and I still hadn't heard more from him.

When Sean and I eventually did meet again, he took me dancing in Hammersmith during the day. I believed the intention was for it to be lessons, but it turned out we'd both done it before, even if it had been a number of years ago, so we ended up staying for a small lunchtime party afterwards.

It was fascinating to see Sean in a social situation. Although I was talking to a group of ladies on one end of the hall, Sean was mingling with a friendship circle, making the men and women laugh. The people around me couldn't help but mention how handsome he was – a good dancer, too – and claimed that I should snap him up before anyone else did.

I wasn't in it for the competition.

All I wanted was a friend.

But that didn't seem to matter much as the weeks went by. We began to see each other more and more, although I still hadn't introduced him to Hayden. Sean didn't press me on the matter either, adhering to his previous promise that this would be completely at my own pace.

Eventually, the guilt crept in. I started to feel bad for how kind and patient he was, constantly having the conversation with myself about how I needed to move on at some point. Sean was the perfect man, for me at least, but it was still tricky to navigate my feelings for Nick. After all, he'd only been gone for eighteen months. It's not long in the grand scheme of things.

One night, I finally trusted my friend's younger sister, Chloe, to babysit Hayden while we had a real date. It was intentionally romantic, which made me feel like I was doing something wrong, but I knew the world wouldn't implode if we only kissed.

The problem was it went further than that.

I ended up at Sean's flat for a while. You know how the story goes — it starts with coffee, leads to a kiss on the sofa, and before you know it, you're acting against your own values and beliefs. Sean and I slept together that night, which was mostly to prove to myself that I could actually go through with it. I tried not to feel bad towards the memory of Nick.

But I enjoyed that night thoroughly.

I don't really know what happened in the weeks after that – whether we were becoming an item or not – but we definitely spent a lot of time together. We were becoming close, however you wanted to label it. Before I knew it, I was figuring out how to move us forward.

In all the romance, I totally forgot about Ryan.

Maybe that was why I liked it so much.

Chapter 26

Now

MY HEAD IS SPINNING. My breath is caught in my throat.

How did I not see this before? Ryan has his mother's eyes, his father's build and chiselled features. I always thought he came from money, and now I'm starting to question just how much it costs to live out here. They own their cottage and are comfortably retiring. It's their home – their hiding place away from the woes of the world. That gets me thinking.

Has Ryan been hiding out here this whole time?

He couldn't have. There are no phones, and the mobile reception out here is non-existent. But that's not to say he didn't move out here after making that threat to me. The thing I'm having trouble with is the coincidence that he would be in the one place I won a break to.

Then it hits me, and I feel like an idiot for believing it in the first place.

Ryan must have made the prize, knowing I'd bite.

My blood is so cold it feels like I'm dead, or at least dying. Hayden is in the next room with Jeanie. She doesn't yet know that I've seen the photos, so I could try to play it cool – to act as though I have no idea anything is wrong.

That I trust her.

I return to the living room with a soft smile – not too much, because I have just been chased by a killer – and sit beside Hayden. He's sipping his hot chocolate now, only stopping to work the marsh-mallows out with the spoon. Jeanie and I watch him adoringly, but my mouth has gone dry as I try to think about how I can edge my way out.

Right into Ryan's hands.

I know we're damned if we do and damned if we don't, but for as long as we're in here, we're sitting ducks. If Jeanie so much as suspects I found those photos, then she'll probably have no issue opening the door and letting Ryan come in to finish me off. I wonder why she hasn't already, but I think I already know why.

They don't want Sean to make it out alive.

He's a loose end.

'I have to say, that does look good.' Turning to face Jeanie, I sigh and then check my watch. Mostly because I can't stand to look at her. 'Do you think Ryan has gone?'

Jeanie simply shakes her head, frowning. 'Don't go out there.'

'We don't really have a choice. That cottage is our home, no matter how temporary, and it's not like we can stay under your roof until Malcolm arrives with the jeep.'

'Please, I insist you do. You're very welcome.'

'But it's not proper.'

She's looking at me like she knows. Or that she thinks *I* know, and she's trying to sound me out. It's a game I don't have time for because who knows where Sean and Malcolm are? Frank could also be back at any moment, so I'm desperate to get out of here and run in literally any direction just to be away from it all.

I'm already willing to give up the act.

'Hayden, we need to leave,' I say softly.

'But there's still some chocolate at the bottom of my mug.'

'I'll make you another one soon, but we have to leave.'

I take the mug from his hand and place it on the table, then stand up and take his hand. Grumpy as an eight-year-old should be when deprived of his sweet treat, he huffs before standing up with me. Jeanie seizes the opportunity to cut off our path.

'You really should stay,' she says. 'It's vital to your survival.'

'Thanks, but I'll make that decision for myself.'

'You're going to get your son killed.'

'And what about *your* son?' I bark.

Jeanie's head snaps back as if I just delivered the most cruel insult on earth. Then her upper lip curves into a sort of snarl, instantly transforming her from sweet old lady to venomous old hag. She puts a leg in our way, but I have youth on my side. I nudge her away with such force that she falls back into her armchair. Earning myself a few seconds, I drag Hayden towards the door, ignoring his protests about going outside with the killer.

It doesn't matter because we're dead either way.

The moment I open the door, Frank and Ryan are standing there with demonic grins on their similar father–son faces. They're blocking the exit, knowing I'm trapped. I let go of Hayden's hand and pull him behind me, shielding him at all costs.

While the killer and his father enter the cottage.

'It's time we had a chat,' Ryan says, sneering. 'Sit down. Now!'

I CAN SEE the end of my life. There's no way out of this without spilling blood, and when I'm surrounded by three people who all want me dead, there's no fighting my way out. All I can do is follow Ryan's instructions and sit.

After all, he's the one with the knife.

But there is one thing I can do. They can't watch me *and* Hayden. Not without splitting up, and it seems as though their nutcase family is stronger as a unit.

'Run,' I whisper to Hayden. 'Find Sean.'

Without so much as a second to waste, he darts between Ryan and Frank, with all that childhood energy to burn as he disappears out the door and into the wild. Frank surprises me by chasing after him, but he stops as soon as he reaches the door, probably not liking his chances. When he turns around, Jeanie asks about Sean, and he shrugs.

That's good, I think.

Both my boys are still alive.

Ryan steps towards me then, letting me see the serrated edge of the hunting knife. I wonder again if it's the one he used on Nick, but then he says something in a low breath that makes me question everything I thought was true.

'I didn't kill Nick,' he says. 'You know that. He was my best friend.'

'But you were happy trying to screw his wife,' I say, regretting it immediately.

'That's not even close to the same level as murder, Kate!'

'You ruined my son's life with that accusation,' Jeanie growls.

'Mum.' Ryan puts up a hand to silence her. Surprisingly, she shuts up and listens while Frank goes to stand with her behind me. Now it's just Ryan and me, his parents becoming mere observers to whatever the hell is about to happen.

The thing is, he could be right. There was always a chance he had nothing to do with the murder at all. But if not him, then who? How can I even find out after five long years?

'Ryan, you need to listen to me,' I say calmly, but I can't hide the frightened urgency in my voice. 'If you didn't kill Nick, then I truly am sorry to have given your name to the police. I'd be angry, too, if I were in your position, but killing me isn't going to fix the situation.'

'Oh yeah?' He grins maniacally. 'What other solution is there?'

'I don't know. Maybe you could turn yourself in to the police and answer their questions. I'm sure they'd understand that you were scared – that you had to go on the run because the evidence was stacked up against you.'

'I wasn't scared!' he snaps. 'I simply knew better than to put myself in handcuffs.'

'Because of the texts?'

'Don't you dare...' He raises a fist to hit me. I wince, but he lowers it. 'Those texts had nothing to do with Nick's death. I give you my word on that. Not that it matters because you've got about five minutes left to live. That's the whole point, Kate. If you're going to label me a killer, I might as well have one very satisfying kill. Why else would I bring you out here?'

So it's true. Ryan really did forge the ticket to lure me into the wilderness. I try not to look shocked, but something still doesn't make sense to me.

'How?' I ask, mostly to stall him so Hayden can get far away from here. 'How did you know I would actually come, and isn't the owner of the cottage going to get wrapped up in the police investigation when we never return?'

Ryan smirks and looks over my shoulder at his parents. They snicker, and then he turns his condescending eyes back to me. 'We *are* the owners of the cottage, stupid. My folks live in one, then rent out the other as a source of income.' He leans in close, his foul breath in my face. 'Nobody knows you're out here. Even Malcolm doesn't know your full names.'

Fear ripples through me as I finally accept my fate. To be honest, I don't entirely blame him for wanting me to suffer. Not if he really is innocent. But that just makes it all the more terrifying, knowing how badly he wants me dead.

'Say a prayer, will you?' he says.

Then, sparing me a final speech, he raises the knife above his head like he did outside. Only this time, he won't miss. One plunge is all it would take.

I close my eyes to accept my inevitable demise at the hands of Ryan Wyatt.

The last thing I see in my mind is my family.

All of them.

I HEAR A SCREAM, thinking it's my own. But it's not. The tone is too light, despite the furious bellow that comes from deep within his gut. I open my eyes just in time to see Hayden springing into the cabin with a thick tree branch in his hands. He swings at Ryan. It thumps against his head with such a blow that he lets out a little yelp and hits the ground beside me. The room goes still, none of us able to believe how hard a young child can swing.

I don't waste any time. There's no sign of Sean or Malcolm, so I rush forward and grab Hayden. He drops the branch and stares at Ryan's stunned, beaten body with his mouth wide open in shock. Snapping him out of it, we run out of the cottage and into the trees.

'You little brat!' Frank yells.

'You'll die for that,' Jeanie adds. 'Both of you!'

I don't have time to see if Ryan is dead, but I don't care right now. All I want is to get far away from those psychopaths, and the only way to do that is to run right into the dark forest with torrents and aggressive gales hurtling towards our faces.

Hayden trips, cries, and wants to give up. I heave him to his feet, endlessly grateful that he came back to save his mum but also welling up with pride. Without him, I would be a dead woman right now. The least I can do is save him in return.

Ryan survived the attack. I know that because I can hear him screaming from somewhere behind us, but I can't make out the words because Frank is yelling over the top of him while the fierce wind attacks us from between the trees. The mud is wet and slippery, slowing our escape as we try to manoeuvre the impossible terrain.

But where could we hide?

There's nothing but trees and rocks around for as far as the eye can see, but when the moonlight catches something up ahead – something high above the treetops, lurking in the night like a vessel of safety – I know instantly it's our only chance.

'There!' I tell Hayden, and we adjust our heading to reach it.

When we reach the feet of the old watchtower, I don't like the way it's groaning under the strength of the wind. I stand there, staring up at it as

Hayden asks me if it's safe. To tell the truth, I don't know, but it's better than getting stabbed to death.

'It's survived this long,' I say, panting and shivering in the cold. 'There's no reason it won't last another few minutes. We just have to hide until Sean gets here, okay?'

Hayden is petrified of heights, and I can see the challenge in his eyes as I take his hand and lead him to go in front of me. At least if he falls, I'll have a chance at catching him. It's a long way up, and losing our grip would surely kill us.

I don't have time to think about my own fear. Not of heights, nor of the two enraged voices that are growing closer with each passing second. Hayden begins his ascent, and I follow close behind him, wondering how much longer we can stay alive.

Chapter 27
Then

THERE WAS *a small fracture in my developing relationship with Sean, though it took me quite some time to figure out exactly what it was. Even weeks after our first intimate evening, I still hadn't introduced him to my son.*

What I didn't know was why.

Sean was a perfectly good man – almost as good as Nick – but there was still something missing. A reason for not bringing him fully into my life. At first, I thought it was just the discomfort of making myself vulnerable again, but that didn't seem quite right. After all, we were otherwise blossoming as a couple.

I finally worked out what it was while we were having a stroll through the city, our hands linked in an unbreakable bond. Despite everything feeling good and right, it was clear to me then that it simply felt as though he had a secret. Perhaps it wasn't even that – it could just be that he knew something I didn't – but he was getting to know me without me really knowing him. Sure, I understood his affinity for seafood and how much he liked long walks, but I never got to understand why or how he'd come to like those things.

'Are you okay?' he asked as we neared Trafalgar Square. 'You've been quiet.'

'Yeah, it's just... I have some questions for you.'

Sean's brow furrowed as he gave a look of pure concern. He said no more as he led me to sit on the wall near one of the lion sculptures. It didn't bother me that a light drizzle was starting to come in or that my backside was wet from the stone wall.

I just wanted answers.

'Want to ask me some of those questions now?' he asked.

'Maybe in a second. I'm just thinking that I don't really know you as much as I'd like to. You keep asking when you're going to officially meet Hayden, but you have to understand that he's my son. It's not that I don't trust you, but—'

Sean raised a hand, then started to fan it, smil-

ing. 'You don't need to explain why you're protective over your own kid, Kate. In fact, I'd be concerned if you weren't. I don't mean to pressure you about advancing our relationship, so if you have some things you'd like to know, go ahead and ask. I'm open.'

I smiled and looked down at my feet, feeling so lucky for landing a guy who could just expose himself to interrogation like that. But I didn't have any really deep questions for him – just small things I didn't mind knowing.

The first question came to mind, and our bonding began.

'Have you always lived in London?' I asked.

'Yes. More or less. My childhood and teen years were spent in Essex, but I moved into a crappy bedsit in the centre of London as soon as I came of age. I was working all the time just to keep a roof over my head, wasting a few good years without really knowing what I wanted to do with my life. It wasn't until I reached my early twenties that I decided I wanted to become a policeman. It really took me by surprise.'

It hadn't taken long. I already felt like I knew him significantly more than before. Little details like that always went a long way, but considering *the ease with which he'd started to talk about himself, I started craving more. That's not to say I pressed him.*

All I did was let him talk.

'I was coming home from a club one night, and this guy was getting loud and pushy with his girl-friend. I knew they weren't an item because I'd seen her kissing someone else earlier that night. But now we were on a quiet street, and this new guy was showing his true colours. Things easily scared me back then, but the situation demanded that I might have to step up and do something if she even gave a slight sign that she needed help.'

'Did she?'

'Oh yes, and then some. I saw her try to walk away, but he pushed her against the wall and started kissing her neck. She was trying to push him away, but he was a lot stronger. Somehow, she got a glimpse of me across the street and begged me for help. The guy – this makes me sick just thinking about it – must have thought she was begging God or something because he didn't turn around. All he was interested in was getting what he wanted.'

I swallowed hard because I'd been in a similar situation before in my life. Not exactly the same, but

Ryan's constant pressuring had left me feeling hopeless and afraid.

'Anyway, I crossed the street and wrapped my arm around his neck. Bear in mind I always hated violence, but I've been a big bloke ever since I hit puberty. So the fella came down to the floor under my strength. The mistake I made was to let go then, thinking that would be enough to talk him out of whatever he wanted to do. Dumb, I know.

'So the man got up, swung a punch right here.' Sean taps his temple. 'It knocked the hell out of me, putting me on the floor in a pathetic heap. The girl ran off, of course, crying and trying to get as far away from the situation as she could. I didn't blame her because her safety was what had brought me into the mess in the first place. Not that it stopped the beating.'

I winced as a storm broke overhead. 'You got hurt?'

'Yeah, he beat me within an inch of my life. See this scar?' He pulled down the front of his T-shirt and pointed to a scar I'd noticed every time we'd ever had sex, but I was always too polite to ask about it. 'That's where he used a broken bottle and stabbed me in the chest. This bloke had some severe anger issues, as you can probably figure out.'

I nodded, not wanting to interrupt.

'As it turned out, the girl didn't just run home. She'd gone to the nearest policeman and brought him back with her. He and his partner arrived on the scene just as that shard of glass was about to go into my throat. They stopped him, wrestled him to the ground, then arranged an ambulance to take me to the hospital.

'I spent a lot of time in that hospital bed, thinking about those officers and how they saved my life. They were so formal and blunt, acting as though it was a normal part of their everyday lives. When I insisted that I'd be dead if it weren't for them, they told me I was the real hero. That was something I'd never heard before, but I liked the way it sounded.

'For months on end, I thought about those cops and how helpful they'd been. Then I thought about how I'd saved that girl – not as a hero, but as a civilian trying to do good. It got me wondering how I could put myself in a position to do even more good. Until it finally struck me that the answer was there all along: I had to become a policeman.'

A smile broke out on my face. I reached for his hand, as he'd done to me so many times. I knew how comforting it was, but I was also over the moon because now I knew something deep and personal about this man. He'd made himself vulnerable to tell me a story, and I would appreciate that for the rest of my life.

'Sorry, I rambled on a bit there.'

'Yeah, you could have trimmed that fat a little.'

We both laughed. Sean kissed my hand and then put an arm around me. I told him there were no more questions for now, and then he smiled, tilting his head back to look up at the dark, murky clouds lingering above us.

'It's going to get heavy,' he said. 'We should make a move.'

I nodded and stood up with him, a familiar sensation flooding through me. Was it love, trust, or just intimately knowing a human being again? Whatever it was, I felt like it was finally time to strengthen our relationship in a way that showed true understanding.

'Come on,' I said. 'Let's go and meet my son.'

WE STOOD *outside the doors of playschool with all the other parents who were waiting to see their kids. Sean held my hand, and I felt how clammy it was. It* meant he was nervous, which was a good thing as far as I saw because it meant he cared.

'Is this okay?' he asked, raising our hands. 'Would it be too much for him to take all at once, with meeting for the first time? It might make him feel like his dad is being replaced.'

I told him he was right and that it was a good idea I wished I'd thought of. Then I let go, and we continued to wait while standing beside each other, almost as if we were merely friends. It was surprising just how much that feeling shook me – I didn't want to be just friends.

Not any more.

The doors opened, and the toddlers came bounding out. Some of the parents went in to search for their kids, but Hayden always knew where to find me. As much as I liked protecting him, it was nice to give him a sense of independence. Anyway, it wasn't like he could wander far.

When he saw me, his eyes lit up as they always did. He tottered my way with his Spider-Man back-pack bouncing behind him and a large, colourful sheet of paper in one hand. I knelt to greet him, kissing him all over his cheek and making him giggle.

'Did you have fun?' I asked as he nodded. 'What's this?'

'A police car.'

I studied the hand-drawn car that, of course, looked nothing like it should. The shapes were far off, the vibrant colours looking like an exploding rainbow, but his effort – as always – was a hundred and ten per cent.

'You know who this is?' I said, pointing at present company, then used the painting as a bridge between these two perfect strangers, whispering in my son's ear. 'This is my friend Sean. He's a police-man, which means he gets to drive a police car.'

Hayden's eyes nearly bulged out of his skull, his mouth wide open before it crept into a smile. Sean knelt beside me, putting himself on the same level as a four-year-old. Well, the best he could do, consid-ering how tall he was.

'Hello there, young man. Did I hear you like police cars?'

'Yeah!'

'Then maybe if your mum will allow it, I can take you for a ride in one. How does that sound?'

I hadn't seen Hayden that happy since before his father passed away. He turned to me as if to seek permission, which I had no problem giving because *it would bring the two halves of my world together. Hayden then screeched with excitement and ran circles around us. I could tell Sean felt a little awkward, so I had to assure him.*

'It's just what kids are like,' I said. 'They have the attention span of a goldfish.'

Only two days later, Sean made good on his promise by arriving at our flat in full uniform, offering to take Hayden out in the car. I was free to go as well, which was good because my son was never going to leave my sight until he could take care of himself. So we went, enjoying the cruise as Sean let Hayden activate the siren. Maybe he would get in trouble for that – I didn't know how those things worked – but I didn't care.

Sean had instantly won him over.

They became best friends in no time, but the relationship stayed exactly there. They were only friends, not father and son, not stepfather and stepson. As Sean and I grew closer, I began to wonder if that connection was going to stand the test of time. But given how Sean always went above and beyond to ensure we were happy, there wasn't a doubt in my mind.

This was going to work out just fine.

Chapter 28
Now

I NEVER QUITE UNDERSTOOD WHY, but that memory of Sean always comforted me. Perhaps it was the way he trusted me, giving himself to me completely as if I were the one who would take care of him. I have that same relationship with Hayden, except I was always destined to be my son's guardian. Whereas with Sean, I lean into him the same way he leans into me.

Where is he now, I wonder?

It's been a few minutes since we climbed the watchtower. I haven't dared remove my weight from the trapdoor we just closed because there's no lock on it – Ryan and Frank could climb up here at any minute, and there's nowhere else to run.

So I sit, and I stay, with Hayden slowly starting

to relax in my arms while I stroke his hair. He's such a big, brave boy, just like his dad. I never expected he would risk his life to come and save me, but I'm so glad he did. Even if I'm still destined to die tonight, at least I get to spend these final few minutes with him, just the two of us and the high, freezing winds.

'Are you doing okay?' I ask softly, his head rolling into my lap.

'I just want to go home.'

'Me too, sweetheart. Me too.'

'Do you think they'll come up here?'

'I honestly don't know. They—'

I don't like where my mind goes next. For as long as I'm sitting on the door, there's nothing they can do to gain entry. But that doesn't mean Ryan's razor-sharp hunting knife can't penetrate the door. There are only three or four inches of solid wood between us and the ladder. What if he decides to start stabbing? If Hayden doesn't get sliced up, then one of my legs is bound to. Then we'd be completely screwed.

'What are you thinking about?' Hayden asks, recognising the alarm in my eyes.

'Nothing. Do me a favour, will you?' I lift him up and get on my knees, peering through the glass in the watchtower's office. 'I'm just going to take a look inside. All you need to do is sit and watch the ladder.'

'No. Wait. I can't open—'

'Hey, *I'll* open it and make the first check. There's no way they can get up here before you manage to close the door again. So just sit here and watch. As soon as you see them, shout to me, and I'll be there in a heartbeat. Okay?'

Hayden hesitates, then nods and moves aside. I take a deep breath, knowing damn well that either one of those maniacs could be hanging on up the top of the ladder, just biding their time until I grant them access. But when the door opens, nobody is there. I can't see the bottom through the darkness, but I can see vague motion. Enough time to search, maybe, with Hayden on lookout and a small sprinkle of luck.

I entrust him with that task and walk around the small office up the top. As soon as I round the corner, the aggression of the wind doubles, its icy hands smacking me all over my bare skin. My teeth grind together while I go for the door, praying it's unlocked and then finally gaining liberation in the warm interior. Well, not warm, but warmer.

It's dark and dusty, unused for a very long time.

There are two desks with scattered paper all over them. I take a step towards the nearest one, but the wood creaks so loud under my foot that I start to question the integrity of this tower. Is it even safe to be up here? Judging by the way it's swaying, I'd say probably not.

Factoring in the psychos down below, I'd say *definitely* not.

The floorboards must be stronger closer to the wall, so I stay as close to it as possible while exploring the dark interior. When I finally reach the first desk, I find the drawers are empty, and there's nothing helpful inside. The other desk has a radio on top of it – an old, rusted one that I can finally see now that I'm closer. I swallow my fear and step across to test it, hoping just one thing could go well tonight. Otherwise, we're stuck in the middle of nowhere, and the Wyatt family *will* see us dead. That's if the freezing temperatures don't get us first.

'Mum!'

A high, panicked voice. Shrill beyond all belief. The scream of sheer horror from a child. I ignore the weak floorboards and sprint across them, hearing one of them snap just as my foot leaves it.

Ignoring the close call, I run for the door as Hayden shouts again.

'They're coming up!'

MY FEET TAKE CONTROL, making rapid leaps across the floorboards until I'm at the trapdoor. Hayden leaps back, his lip quivering with raw fear as I peer down at the ladder. Ryan and Frank are both there, rapidly making their ascent to us.

I slam the door shut and kneel on it, yelling at Hayden to head inside, watch his step, and grab anything he can find – anything at all, as long as it looks heavy enough to barricade a door. Until then, I'm stuck on top of it while Ryan bashes up at it with his fists.

'Open it now, Kate, and get what's coming to you!'

At least that's what I think he says. It's hard to hear over the deafening roar of the wind that's so cold it's making my eyes water. Or is that pure dread making me cry? All I know for sure is that I can't let them in because then it will be all over.

The pressure intensifies when the banging doubles. The trapdoor lifts up as if Frank has joined him somehow, putting their strength together to get us. I grab hold of the railing and use that to push myself down, planting my knees in while Ryan lets out a guttural roar.

'I'm not messing around here. You're only making it worse!'

The trapdoor drops, closing again instantly. I almost face-plant the wood, it happens so fast. There's silence then, and it makes me wonder what they're up to. I sit up slightly, just enough to see movement behind the glass, desperately searching for something to help us.

Then my worst fears come to life.

The first stab misses my knee by half an inch. It pierces the wood with no trouble at all, wooden splinters flying up before the wind carries them away in the bat of an eye. I freeze, knowing I can't move because then they'll simply enter and kill us.

Ryan retracts the knife. There's a second of peace before he strikes again, this one nicking my shin, probably drawing blood, but it's too dark to tell. I whimper quietly, not letting him know he's got me, then shift my position while trying my best not to cry.

Once more, the knife disappears. Three quick stabs slice through the wood, not as far through but just as lethal. I stand up then, putting my feet on the corners and knowing they can be pierced by that enormous knife at any second. I don't know how much longer I can hold on.

Seconds, if I'm lucky.

Hayden appears at my side, looking proud of himself as he holds a stepladder lengthways in his tiny arms. I stare at him for a moment, dumbfounded that he thinks this will help. Then I see what he's thinking – that it's not about weight at all.

It's about brains.

'You're a little genius,' I say as he hands me the ladder.

Without a second to lose, I slide the far end under the rail, wedging it between the corner of the office wall and the lowest bar on the fence. It tucks in nicely, the rest of the ladder stretching across the trapdoor before I tuck it under the railing on the other side. Ryan tries again to stab through the wood, striking the metal ladder and yelling with impatience.

'What the hell are you doing up there, Kate? Let us up!'

He gives up with the knife and tries once again to use brute force to open it. Hayden and I sit on the horizontal ladder, adding weight to this strategy and reinforcing the barricade. The door doesn't move, no matter how hard that loony and his father try.

Eventually, Ryan gives up. Hayden and I are left holding each other, our breaths rapid and hot. Our eyes aren't leaving the door because we fear this may be a trick to make us come down. But nothing will make us leave this tower, not for as long as Sean is out there finding help. Until he does, this is the one place we're completely safe.

For now, at least.

IF I KNEW this was how I would die, I never would have taken this trip.

It'd started as a free ticket, but now my son and I are stuck at the top of an abandoned watchtower. There's nobody around for miles, save for the people on the ground trying to kill us. We haven't heard a peep from them in a few minutes, but they're still there.

They must be.

Hayden is snuggled into me, the pale moonlight drawing attention to the tears on his cheeks. He finished crying a while ago, but they're still there, crystallising under his raw eyes. I wipe them away with my thumb, still pressing my foot hard onto the trapdoor that leads to the only ladder. He's looking at me like I can save him, but I'm not sure I can.

'It's going to be okay,' I say to him.

But that's a lie. We're only slightly higher than the trees that surround us, and the nearest town is so far away I can't even see it from here. Sean went for help a long time ago, and he should be back by now. It's time I start accepting that we're going to die.

It quickly becomes a reality when I start to smell smoke. It's creeping up the ladder and seeping through the trapdoor. At first, I thought it was my mind playing a nasty trick on me, but when I start to cough, I realise with absolute certainty that our pursuers are going to get us – that they've started a fire to smoke us out, and the only way out is down.

One way or another, we're going to die.

Or are we?

I leap to my feet, trying hard not to let Hayden know I'm panicking as much as he is. There has to be a way out – *has* to be. There is one thing we can do, but there's a great risk of casualty if we dare to be so bold. I look at my son, then at the trees.

He knows what I'm thinking.

'Mum, we can't.'

'We might have to.'

'But if we fall, we'll die.'

'If we stay here, we'll die anyway.'

That silences him, and I know it's because he's scared stiff. I examine the trees again, judging that we can make it onto one of the larger branches if only we dare to take one large step. The branch is wet – that's the real trouble – as well as swaying in the growing gale. We could make it, maybe, as long as we have the courage to do so.

Now the winds are carrying the smoke out of the forest, lifting it high and spewing it onto the breeze like a signal. It keeps us from coughing, for now at least, but the intense heat is growing. There's no way of telling just how long we can stick it up here, but the forest below is glowing amber, like a cigar's tip as it burns away, slowly killing its smoker.

The same way this will kill us.

'Take my hand,' I tell Hayden, preparing to lead my own child into the most dangerous thing he'll ever do. He shakes his head, then starts to reach out. Then he freezes, as if coming to his senses. When he takes a final glance over the railing and sees the watchtower legs slowly consumed by the blaze, he knows time is of the essence.

He takes my hand, and we challenge death.

Together.

Chapter 29
Then

ANOTHER EIGHTEEN MONTHS WENT PAST, *and Sean was a part of the family. We'd discussed the idea of finding a house together, laying down a large deposit on a mortgage if we couldn't outright buy it. But I had an emotional attachment to the flat I'd been living in, and it was big enough for the three of us anyway, so I suggested he move in with us.*

It took a while to completely sell him on the idea because he didn't want to intrude on Nick's legacy. Even so, he eventually came around on the condition he could pay towards the mortgage. When I told him we owned the flat and there was no need to pay, his jaw dropped at how fortunate we were to have such a home to call our own.

There was no way he could afford this place anyway.

As soon as he moved in, it felt only slightly uncomfortable. We had to shift things around so he wasn't simply sleeping on Nick's side of the bed, his clothes filling up his wardrobe and generally just acting as a substitution. After some time, it started to feel like a new life where we could develop our relationships as a family.

I told him I loved him, too.

It came out surprisingly easily, when I saw him playing with Hayden on the carpet. It'd always come so naturally to him, accepted by my son with no hiccups whatsoever. So when I blurted out how I felt about him, he simply smiled and then told me he also loved me.

We lived in bliss, me acting as a housewife while Sean went out to continue his career as a policeman. Hayden was six then, going to school each day all by himself. Well, not completely by himself – a large group of friends walked to and from the school together so they could keep each other safe. I loved that he was protected, but I hated the worry it caused me.

One day, while Sean and I were having a sneaky afternoon smooch in the kitchen – the dinner hissing in the background as smoke started to rise from the pan – Hayden came bursting into the flat. We greeted him merrily as always, taking our hands off each other, but were shocked to see him storm into his bedroom and slam the door.

'What was that all about?' Sean asked.

'I have no idea. Can you watch the food for a minute?'

'No problem.'

I rapped on Hayden's door, ignored the fact he told me to go away, then let myself in. My son was lying face down on the bed, sobbing into his arms. I went to him, perching by his feet and putting a loving hand on his back.

'What's wrong, sweetheart?'

'Nothing. Go away.'

It was hard not to take it personally, but this growing boy was clearly upset about something. I slid closer to him, gently pulling his arm away from his face. He tried to turn his head, but by then, I'd already seen what was causing the trouble.

The red mark around his eye was already bruising.

I held back a gasp, shocked that somebody would dare hurt my precious son. But I had to display complete calmness, with no judgement or explosive reaction on my part. It was imperative that I listened, waiting for him to tell me who'd done this to him.

'Let me take a look at that,' I said, easing his arm away. He let me do it this time, maybe because I was showing myself to be smooth and easy-going. It looked worse on a second glance, the bruise almost reaching his temple. 'Come on. Let's get a cold pack on it.'

'Will it help?' he asked, the threat of tears croaking in his throat.

'It'll reduce the swelling at the very least.'

We went into the kitchen, where Sean happily greeted him. I signalled behind Hayden's back that he should shush, as if to say that he wasn't to make a big deal of it. Without me even asking, Sean took a bag of peas from the freezer, knelt, and pressed it against Hayden's face.

He hissed at the sudden cold.

'It's okay, buddy,' Sean said, soothing him. 'That's quite a shiner. What happened?'

'Someone was picking on my friend, so I pushed him.'

'Let me guess, he swung for you a second later?'

'Yeah.'

'This looks like a big-boy bruise. Was he bigger than you?'

'Way bigger.'

'Then I'm proud of you for sticking up for your friend.'

The kitchen was quiet then, save for the mumblings of Sean telling him to keep the peas pressed against his eye. Hayden complained that it stung, so I started making a cup of hot chocolate to distract him from the pain. It was tough not to freak out at the fact an older kid had left a mark like that on my son, but Sean gave me the look – the one that said I didn't need to worry because he was going to handle it.

And I believed him.

A WEEK WENT BY. The bruise was starting to look less angry, the swelling subsiding as the red turned to pink. Thanks to Sean's wise words, he was starting to wear it like a badge of honour. Bad things happened to good people, was what had been explained to him, and sometimes you just had to stand up tall and proud, announcing that fear won't beat you down. I liked the message but hoped it wouldn't lead to more violence.

I was now in the habit of walking him to and from school myself. Hayden didn't love that, but I didn't want that kid jumping him in the street. If anything had been proved at that point, it was that safety in numbers was a fallacy.

That's why I insisted on going.

Upon picking him up in the afternoon, I caught his teacher moving between buildings. Hayden told me I didn't need to speak to her, but I dismissed it as typical kid behaviour, trying not to make a big deal out of it so I didn't embarrass him. It made me feel a little bad, but this whole thing had to be sorted. Mostly because I was sick of worrying.

'Mrs. Norris?' I called.

The teacher spun around with one of those fake, aren't-I-lovely smiles. She barely looked old enough to be a teacher, her skinniness and youthful face working with her auburn hair to play down her age. Some people were just plain lucky with their appearance.

'Can I speak with you a second?' I asked. 'It's about Hayden's eye.'

'Oh. Has there been a development?'

My face creased up with confusion. 'No, I mean I want the kid punished.'

'Sorry, I don't understand. I thought it was dealt with?'

I wasn't sure what exactly was going on, so I looked down at Hayden. He was looking the other way, trying to be invisible by the looks of it. It wasn't working.

'Hayden, do you know anything about this?'

'Yeah,' he said, then looked up at me. 'Sean spoke with Mrs. Norris. The bully and his parents were there. They made him apologise to me and promise he won't do it again.'

'Oh. Well...' I felt stupid, not knowing what to say. I'd come into this preparing for things to perhaps get a little heated. Imagine my surprise when I found out it'd already been resolved. 'I guess my partner forgot to tell me,' I said to Mrs. Norris.

'That's all right. Is there anything else I can help you with?'

I told her no, thanked her for her time, then began to walk Hayden back to our Marylebone home. We had a little time to talk, during which I pressed my son for more information regarding the resolution of his school playground debate. He had little more to offer, only repeating the same thing over and over again.

'Sean sorted it out.'

I couldn't work out why Sean hadn't said anything to me. It wasn't like me to play the parent card, but Hayden was my son, and I felt like I had a right to know about every little affair in his life. Why had he kept it from me? How was I supposed to feel about it?

Sean was the only person I could ask.

I KEPT *the thought to myself for as long as possible, enjoying our evening as a family. It was important that Hayden saw us as a family unit, and on the slim chance this would turn into some kind of argument, I wanted to do this in private.*

Late that night, when he was in bed, Sean and I started to turn in ourselves. It'd been a long day for us both – him working thirteen hours and me cleaning the entire flat from top to bottom, plus handling both the school runs. It's safe to say we were equally exhausted, which made this a bad time to bring it up.

Unfortunately, there was no better time.

'Can I talk to you about something?' I asked.

Concern registered on Sean's face as he lifted the duvet and slid into bed. I did the same, but we both sat up and looked at each other, using propped-

*up pillows to lean against. The dimly lit room repre-
sented how I felt; gloomy.*

'What's wrong?' he asked softly.

*'I spoke to Hayden's teacher today. About the
black eye.'*

'Oh, that.'

*'Yes. That. She says the whole matter has been
resolved by none other than yourself. What
happened? Why didn't you tell me about this?'*

*Sean sighed and adjusted his position, tugging
the pillow around and struggling to find a comfortable spot. 'I went in and spoke to the headteacher
the very next day, in full uniform so I could exercise
my authority a little. They took the issue very seriously and called the boy's parents in the same day.
We all sat in a room together and resolved it within
minutes.'*

*I couldn't believe what I was hearing. 'You
mean all the parents sat around and discussed why
my son was beat up, but I – his own mother –
wasn't invited? Sean, that's not nearly good enough.
Even if you didn't invite me, you could've at least
told me.'*

'I'm sorry. Truly, I am.'

*That was all he said, not offering the slightest
explanation as to why he'd kept me out of it. Like he*

was going to make me dig, and I wasn't afraid to do so.

'Right,' I said. 'So go on, tell me why you kept this to yourself.'

'I just didn't want you to worry. This whole parenting thing is brand new to me. You've had six years to figure it all out, but I kind of found myself in the deep end. I moved in with a widow, had to play the father figure without treading on Nick's memory, and I had no experience with either.' He took my hand, and I let him. 'I'm so sorry for not telling you. Would it help if you knew what was going on in my head?'

'A little.' I shrugged.

'You're a good mum – great, in fact – but you worry a lot. I was thinking that you worry so much about what happened with Nick, you can't relax when Hayden is out of your sight. It hurts to watch because I desperately want you to be happy. So I took it upon myself to repair the situation, taking the entire weight so you wouldn't have to. It was quick, clean, and smooth. Done in just a few short hours with a full apology and a grounding.'

I watched him, studying his face and wondering if there was a lie in there somewhere.

There wasn't.

'Every day, I thought about telling you,' he went on. 'But you were always worried about the next thing. You didn't mention the black eye again, so I thought you'd just let it slip. I was just trying to keep you both safe and happy. I didn't realise you needed to know, so I'm very truly sorry, from the bottom of my heart.'

The apology was undeniably sincere. Everything, from the soft tone to the shame in his eyes, contributed to my belief that he'd only been trying to do the right thing. I told myself it was just a mistake and that he was trying to navigate the treacherous waters of parenthood as much as I was, only he had no experience in the subject.

But I did appreciate him trying. I told him so, thanking him for resolving the problem in its entirety. Although there were more mistakes to make along the way, I felt completely safe knowing that – no matter where we went or what we faced – Sean would always have my back. He would forever go above and beyond to keep me and my son safe.

That was a guarantee.

Chapter 30
Sean

Malcolm drives them up the hill, the two officers in the back, while Sean sits up front, feeling more anxious than ever before in his life. The headlights barely break the night, only briefly lighting up the trees before the vehicle bounces and shifts its heading. They all hold on for dear life while the driver does the best he can in such harsh conditions.

One of the officers speaks of a fire, requesting services to help contain a blaze. Sean's ears prick up at this. He turns, sees the cop is using his radio, then returns his attention to the front, leaning forward to see the sky.

Shock steals through him when he spots it.

Thick plumes of smoke are reaching for the bleak, night-time clouds. Flashes of embers light up the forest. The chaos seems to be farther than the cottages – somewhere behind, where the jeep may not even reach.

'Fire services?' he asks the officer. 'We'd be lucky to even get up there ourselves.'

'There are means. They're trained for things like this.'

Sean appreciates the gesture of comfort, but he's no fool. He's worked with firemen in the past, arriving on the scene of nightclub fires and working together to control the mayhem. Those men do everything they can to save lives, but it doesn't always work.

How can a forest be any easier?

They sit in silence, the jeep struggling and grumbling and throwing them around. Sean spends the whole time staring up at the flames, wondering what on earth has gone wrong – how much worse things have become since he left Kate and Hayden at the cottage. He can't stop wringing his hands because he once made a promise to keep them safe. It's possible that he's already failed, he realises with glum horror. Even if they're still alive right now, that doesn't mean they still will be by the time help arrives.

There's nothing he can do but sit and wait.

And pray.

Chapter 31
Now

THE FIRE HAS CLIMBED the tower just like we did. Its flames reach up and spread along the wood, spitting and crackling and kicking up smoke. Hayden takes my hand as I cling desperately to the tree. I hold him close while telling him we need to move – that we can't stay here.

'Why?' he asks. 'The flames aren't touching the trees.'

'Yet,' I say.

Far below, Ryan and Frank are standing back and admiring their handiwork. I can only imagine how frustrated they are that we didn't climb down the ladder or even just stay up there and roast. We've made our way safely into the swooning tree, but it won't be long before we both lose our grip and fall.

I look around for the sturdiest tree in sight. I find one right away, not too far from our current position. 'See that one over there, with the two branches that look like arms?' I point into the darkness, the flames licking up at the tower with frightening speed. 'You need to climb over to that *very* carefully.'

'What about you?'

'I'm right behind you.'

Hayden does a fantastic job of holding in his fear, but I have a mother's intuition. I can see the fire in his eyes like I can see his shaking hands reaching out fearfully in the dark for a better grip. He navigates the long, wet branch like young boys do, not looking down because he knows a single glance will kill his confidence and, in turn, him.

As promised, I stay close behind him. My son must have better grip on his shoes than I do because my feet keep slipping. I hear a roar from behind me, not just the wind attacking the tree I'm so painfully hoping will stay upright but a burst of flames quickly reaching the office at the top of the tower. The smoke reaches up and out, making the forest look like the sky above an erupting volcano. I can feel the sweltering heat from here.

I shimmy along, wondering just how we're going to get down. Even if we do make it safely to the next tree, there are still two killers waiting for us on the ground. They got what they wanted – trapping us up here – but there's still distance between us.

Hayden reaches the next tree, then turns and reaches out a hand. Bless his heart for trying to help me, but I won't be able to make it. A swift wind grabs the tree and pushes it sideways, as if trying to shake me from it. I hold on tight and close my eyes as it tilts at an unnatural angle. The bark is wet, my fingers failing to get a good grip.

Then the tree returns to its upright position. I don't know how long we have, but I need to move. I'm about to take the next step when something catches my eye. A light in the distance, but not from the fire. Fires don't fly.

Emergency helicopters do.

Mad laughter erupts from my chest as I realise what's happening. Sean did it – he found help, and now they're coming. He might not be far behind, and God knows where the police are, but that aerial firefighter should be able to dowse the fire before it spreads to the trees. We might just be safe after all, if only we can hold on a moment longer.

But there is a time limit. The weight of that water will knock me from the tree. That's if the fire doesn't get to me first. I hurry along the branch, reaching out for Hayden's hand. We need to get as far away from the flames as possible, so I steel my nerves as my son grabs hold of me, his palm slick with sweat. He's as slippery as the tree, so I freak out, release my grip, and grasp the current branch in a tight bear hug. I'm too scared to let go – even more so to look down because I know what's going to happen.

The helicopter whirls closer, making an attempt against the fire. The wind picks up again in the blustery chaos. I have seconds to get out of this damn tree before it takes me for another long sway. Maybe one I can't hold onto for a second time. It's now or never – I either take the leap or I don't. My survival instinct kicks in, and I reach for Hayden's hand once more.

Only this time, I don't make it.

The wind shifts the tree at the last second. I only have one hand on the branch, which slides out of my grasp. I feel weightless as I'm flung from the tree, the wind tearing at me as I make a final leap to the next branch. But it's useless. I'm not close enough. I close my eyes and scream as gravity takes me. The last thing I see is Hayden.

He's crying as he loses his mother to the fall.

I'M RELIVING that same dreadful moment over and over. Hayden's hand is outstretched, the branch sliding out from under my foot. The final second before I start to fall, my body plummeting towards the ground. I hear his scream over and over, the horror of loss in his eyes.

But still, I fall.

There's no feeling quite like it. The churning of the stomach. The tightening of all your muscles when you know you're going to die. They say your entire life flashes before your eyes, but that's not true – you just see the same image over and over.

Hayden.

Then, out of the black sky comes a beep. It's long and steady, reaching its crescendo before it starts all over again. The whole world is dark, and I see nothing. The beep repeats again and again, quicker this time, my son's name ringing through my head while my entire body screams in an explosion of pain and terror.

My eyes shoot open. It's bright white. My body is numb, and there's a dry, sour taste in my mouth. There are two people leaning over me, both in blue scrubs, as I gasp – one short, desperate wheeze, followed by a thick cough.

'She's awake!' one of them yells.

I'm told to rest – that everything is okay and that my son is safe, but I won't believe it until I see it with my own eyes. I protest in that weak manner, barely able to get the words out as I slip in and out of consciousness. For me, it feels like seconds, but the scene changes every time I open my dry eyes, like a slideshow shifting between images.

Until I find the one I want.

'Sean,' I say in a breath.

He shushes me and takes my hand. I'm anything but calm, although my energy is spent. I look around to find a nurse doing something by the window. Sean asks if we can have a moment alone, and she happily agrees. As soon as she's gone, that one word is on my lips.

'Hayden?'

'He's safe,' Sean says, holding my hand just enough to keep me steady. 'Trust me, he's reading a book in the next room with just a couple of bumps.

You're okay, too. Nothing is broken or out of place. You just took a nasty fall, that's all.'

I look down and see scratches everywhere, deep and red, criss-crossing over my hands and arms. They don't hurt, but they should. Maybe the doctors put something in my body – drugs or whatever it is they do these days. I start to relax, but then something else makes me shoot up, some of the wires pulling at the rapid yanking.

'Ryan! Frank! Are they—'

'It's taken care of,' Sean says soothingly. I know what he's doing. He's altering his tone to keep me mellow, but I don't want mellowness. I want facts. Answers. I know he knows this. 'I got them, Kate. I got the police for you. They found Ryan on the scene, but Frank was the one who'd set fire to the watchtower. Apparently, they're related.'

'Father and son' is all I can get out, my body fatiguing.

'Wow. I guess that makes sense.' Sean huffs out a deep breath, then kisses my hand and puts it gently beside me. Then he leans forward, putting his elbows on his knees and propping his face up with his hands. 'They're with the police now. Jeanie, too. There's a long legal battle ahead, but they're being done for grand arson and attempted murder, at the very least. When we found them, they didn't even know we were there. They were still screaming up at you, threatening to cut you into tiny little pieces. The policemen heard them, too, fortunately.'

'That explains it. How those two were caught, I mean, but what about Jeanie?'

'We found her when we searched the cottages. She had no problem confessing. Crazy old witch thought it would make them go easy on her.' He smiles then, and it seems to glow like it's heavenly or something. 'And you – luckiest person on the planet – got caught between two of the branches on the way down. It knocked you clean out, but at least you didn't have to feel the pain while they called people in to rescue you.'

'Wasn't Deepwood on fire, then?'

'No. They managed to put it out before it spread. They also got Hayden out of there as fast as possible. He's a little rattled, but that's eased up over the past few days.'

'Days?'

'Yes, days. But don't worry. It's all going to be okay now. Just rest.'

I close my eyes and try to process it all: the lucky fall, the arrest of Ryan and his psycho family, my son being rescued from a ridiculously tall tree. We're fortunate enough to have survived, but to have done so while not breaking any bones? We must have a guardian angel. I wonder if it was Nick, looking out for his family from the Great Beyond.

We're also blessed to have had Ryan arrested. After all this time, it's pretty plain to see he didn't kill Nick. No wonder he wanted to hurt me so bad – I wrecked his life with that accusation, and he never did manage to claim it back.

Which, of course, leaves one final question.

Who *did* kill him?

I GROW STRONGER PRETTY FAST, my body healing so rapidly that the doctors have no problems discharging me. They reunite me with Hayden, who cries as he hugs me. It's not like my eyes are dry either – I'm so lucky to have him back safely in my arms.

Outside, where the taxi is pulling up and I'm stuck in a wheelchair as per the doctor's orders, Hayden opens the door and gets ready to escort me in. Sean, however, stays back with me, helping me out of my chair. I start to make a move, but he calls back to me, telling Hayden he just needs a minute to speak with me alone.

'Something's wrong,' he says. 'I can see it in your eyes.'

'That's impressive. I didn't say a word.'

'You didn't need to. I know you.'

The nurse wishes me well and walks off with the wheelchair, leaving us to talk while the taxi driver grows impatient. Sean's right – something *is* horribly wrong – but I don't quite know how to broach the subject. Certainly not here, out in the open.

'As soon as we get the chance,' I whisper, licking my cracked lips and fighting off a monstrous headache, 'we need to talk about something serious. About Nick's murder. There's something you don't know yet, and...'

Sean nods, but he won't look me in the eye. Not right away. By the time he does, there's a smile on his face that says this won't be a problem. As if it was written in the stars for us to at least talk about it. After all, there's a years-old mystery to solve.

'I know' is all he says before helping me into the taxi.

We sit holding each other in the back of the taxi. Hayden is tucking a blanket over me, but I'm already burning alive. Sean helps to make sure I'm okay, but Hayden insists he has it taken care of because he thinks of himself as a man.

But then he says something that somehow warms and chills me at once.

'We can look after her together... Dad.'

Sean smiles from ear-to-ear while I'm still focused on what Sean said: that he knows. I think about it for the next few hours, wondering just what he meant by that. I'm trying not to let it bug me, but there's something deep down inside that just won't let it go. Maybe it's the bump to the head that's making me overthink, so I need to just let it slide for now and focus on the important things right in front of me.

My family and I are safe.

Finally.

Chapter 32
Now

We don't find a good time for the conversation, which makes things very uncomfortable for me. It's like holding a heavy weight, which only seems to get heavier the longer I hold it. I'm desperate to get it over with, and I won't be able to wait much longer.

Tonight might be my chance. It's New Year, and we're at a fancy party hosted by Sean's work colleagues. I never did think being surrounded by policemen would make me feel fidgety and awkward, but here we are. I wonder if it's something to do with being away from Hayden – he's at the flat with Chloe, the babysitter, finally enjoying the PlayStation I bought him a lifetime and a half ago. It wasn't my choice to leave him, but my therapist recommended getting some space if, and *only* if, Hayden felt comfortable with it. I sensed honesty when he said he was happy at home and hated New Year as much as Christmas.

So now I'm standing on the balcony at some shindig, just like back on my wedding day. The room behind me is full of glitter and flashing lights because the officers invited their wives, who took over the party. They're playing a whole bunch of songs from the nineties, throwing me back to my childhood. It's hard to believe I used to be an innocent little kid, and now I'm a mother myself. As I stare out across the magnificent view of London, with the surprisingly warm breeze brushing my cheeks, I get a moment to consider how lucky we are to be alive.

At least the pain is easing already. My hands are lightly scarred from all the branch scratches, and my head still thunders with pain every couple of hours, but I'm able to move around no problem. I can even enjoy a party, for crying out loud. How many survivors of ordeals get to say things like that just days after they almost died?

The papers say we're lucky to have lived at all. I keep seeing stories about me and 'The Widow's Retreat in Deepwood'. It's hard to believe I'm back in the spotlight again after all this time, but hopefully, this will be the end of it. I just want to be left alone.

'May I join you?' a voice asks, interrupting my thoughts.

I turn my head to see Sean standing there in his T-shirt and blazer. His hands are in his trouser pockets, making him look relaxed and casual. A member of staff walks around with champagne flutes on a tray, and he takes two of them with a smile. Then he hands one to me and joins me without waiting for an answer.

Because of course he can join me.

I love him.

'Here's to the people who are missing,' he says, raising his glass.

'Cheers.'

We clink glasses, and I think not only of Nick but of my mother. I wonder what she would make of this whole situation if she were still around. I can sort of picture her standing next to me, prattling on in my ear about how I need to do a better job at parenting. It makes me feel a little guilty for remembering how she always used to be rather than the person I grew to like – maybe even love – in her final days.

I want to distract myself, but it's hard to enjoy the party when there are such serious matters at hand. Like I said, it's New Year, which means we get a chance to start over. I'd like one of my resolutions to be 'no more lies'. In order to do that, I need to get something off my chest. But I'm not going to do that here. It's too open. Too suffocatingly busy.

All I have to do is blurt it out.

'Sean, I'd like to talk about Nick now.'

'You mean...?'

'Yes, what we started to discuss back at the hospital.'

His face droops into a worried frown. It looks as though he's about to get upset with me, but then he knocks back the entire glass of champagne and hisses through his teeth as the bubbles work on him. 'Do you want to do it here? With all these people?'

'No. Could we maybe leave? I'm worried about Hayden anyway.'

'You don't want to wait for the ball to drop?'

'Not really. But we can stay if you want to.'

Sean rubs my arms and tells me it's okay – that I should finish my drink while he gets our coats. Then he leaves me on the balcony for a couple of minutes, letting me soak in that last breath of fresh, high-altitude air. It's peaceful. Bliss.

But a storm is coming.

Sean returns with our coats, helping me into mine and then escorting me through the hall. Plenty of people stop us, giving him grief for being a party pooper. He laughs it off and explains that we're not feeling great, a lie that comes from his mouth so naturally. I wonder what else he lies about, but maybe that's just me projecting.

Just because I'm a liar, it doesn't mean everyone is.

When we finally get downstairs, it's a lot easier to hear each other. We begin our walk home, taking a nice, quiet stroll down the more peaceful streets. There are people everywhere, yelling excitedly and knocking back drinks, singing as they head towards the next bar. They're having a great time, and that's great for them.

But I feel miserable.

It's my nerves, really, and this is something I deserve. Reap what you sow, isn't that what they say? Is that why we're making small talk for our entire journey, as though I'm backing out of what I previously committed to? The things I need to say won't be easy to hear, and they sure as hell won't be easy to say. But they *do* need to be said.

Tonight.

We get too close to home, and I know my last chance is here. I stop in the street and look around, loving how quiet it's suddenly become. It also surprises me to see the Paddington Street Gardens are open at this time of night. It must be a special exception for New Year's Eve.

'Could we take a short stroll and finally get to it?' I ask.

Sean nods and takes my hand. I wonder if he thinks I'm going to reveal I've cheated on him or something like that. I want to put his mind at ease, but what I have to say is far worse than that. I've been dishonest for so long that cheating would probably seem like a good thing compared to this. I'm not sure if it's the alcohol or my discomfort making me sweat.

We find an empty bench and take a seat. Sean tries to keep hold of my hand, but I need to wring my fingers and face him. I look into his eyes and hold his gaze, telling him it's okay if he doesn't want to be with me after this. That I'll understand.

'You're starting to scare me,' he says. 'This is about Nick, right?'

I nod, my mouth suddenly bone dry. I move my tongue around, as if tasting the words before they leave my lips. There's no way out of this now – it's now or never, all or nothing. I need to throw myself into the deep end and just blurt it out.

'I wasn't entirely honest about the wedding fire,' I say.

Sean's expression doesn't change. He just looks at me, waiting for more.

'The truth is, I was looking around that night. I saw a guest accidentally knock a candelabra, and it hit the tablecloth. The fire spread, catching the chairs, the curtains, and so on. When I said in my statement that it was one of the things leading me to think Ryan was my husband's killer, I was...' A deep sigh to clear my lungs. 'I was lying. It wasn't him.'

There's silence for a moment, and then Sean rests a hand on my shoulder, rubbing gently with his thumb. 'That's okay. You knew how bad a person he was and that he was doing all sorts of crazy things. Sometimes your mind just fills in the blanks to implicate someone. It's how we humans work. Like when you saw Ryan flee the scene after doing what he did.'

I shake my head, my heart beating frantically. 'That's another thing I lied about.'

Sean tilts his head to the side, wrinkling his forehead.

'The figure I saw running up the street... It wasn't Ryan.'

'You already told me you didn't see his face.'

'But I didn't see his face because – oh God, this is awful.' I breathe deeply, battling my anxiety, then press on against the strain. 'Because there was no face to see. Whoever killed Nick did it without leaving a single trace of evidence except what you found on the security tape. Found, then destroyed.' I bury my hands in my face as tears start leaking from my eyes. My shoulders heave as the sobbing begins.

But Sean takes my hands gently and hits me with the big news.

'I know,' he says. 'Remember when I said it before – that I know?'

'What—' an interrupting sniffle '—are you talking about?'

'When you told me about that night, I told you I already knew. Then, back at the hospital, you said you had to talk about Nick. Something serious, you said, and I once again told you I knew. I wasn't just agreeing with you – it was my way of saying you don't need to worry any more. Because I already know the truth. All of it.'

I study his eyes, the knowing smile pulling up the corners of his lips. My crying slows down, my body restless as I try to decipher his meaning. Does he truly know? No. He can't. It's impossible because he's a policeman.

And I would already be in prison.

'I know you killed Nick,' he says.

'That's not—'

'You don't need to pretend any more, Kate. I've known all along, and your secret is safe.' He pauses, probably expecting me to either deny it or express my undying gratitude. When he doesn't get what he wants, he goes on. 'There *was* no man on the security footage because there was no man. There's been talk all around the investigation about the trajectory of the stabs. They matched that of a woman at exactly your height. I've spent years leading my colleagues astray, misguiding them and tampering with evidence. It's okay.'

The park has gone deadly silent and freezing cold. I shiver, wrap my arms around my stomach as my nerves all shoot off like fireworks. My foot starts bobbing up and down of its own accord. 'What do you mean, *evidence*?'

'I mean all of it. The knife you tried to hide in the lobby's bin. Nick's phone that has proof of his infidelity with all those other women. My, he did like to get around, didn't he? No wonder you wanted him dead so badly.'

'Hey, I didn't—'

'The phone is gone, so you don't have to worry. It went into the River Thames that night, along with the security footage from the building across the street.'

My mouth hangs open.

'You didn't know about that one, did you?' Sean shakes his head and tuts. 'It shows you bringing a blood-soaked blanket into the lobby and feeding it into the bin. If you slow it down enough, you can actually see the knife leave the blanket. It was sloppy work, my love. But like I said, it's taken care of. Your secret is safe.'

I don't know what to say. Not only has he figured everything out, but he knew it all along. All those lies I told for all those years, there was somebody who knew I was a killer. He knew I was angry about Nick's cheating and that I wanted the inheritance so I could live without him or any other care in the world. Which also means he knew—

'Ryan is innocent,' he says, like he can read my mind. 'Well, that's a very loose term because he tried to kill you, but he didn't kill Nick. No wonder he's angry. But, like you keep drawing attention to, the guy is a piece of work and needs to be punished. If he has to take the fall so we can be together, that's fine by me.

'I love you, Kate. I have from the very moment I first saw you. When I was in your flat on the night of the murder – when you lied to the police about what happened. That's why I started following you, watching you from behind the scenes until the right moment came. Did you think it was an accident that I found you in the supermarket all that time ago? I planned it, my love. I took fate into my own hands, and here we are.'

There's a different side of Sean now – like he's a man I never really knew. I start piecing it together in my head: hiding the evidence, misleading the police, and then approaching me in the supermarket. He was obsessed with me, and it makes me shiver violently.

Sean tells me there's nothing to worry about – that he'll keep my secret for as long as we're together. I realise it's a type of blackmail, not unlike the kind Ryan had pressed on me five years ago. There's no choice but to stay with Sean now. I can't get angry because he'll spill the beans and lock me up for years. Hayden will be motherless, and really, he's the only thing I ever cared about in this world.

So I'll stay. For as long as I need to, Sean and I will remain a happy, blessed couple without any obstacles or strife. I don't need to fear him because I've seen the extent he'll go to in order to protect us. Hayden and I are safe in his capable hands, and I trust him fully.

But if he ever crosses me, just like Nick did with all those women?

God help him.

For other books by AJ Carter, visit:

www.ajcarterbooks.com/books

About the Author

AJ Carter is a psychological thriller author from Bristol, England. His first book, *The Family Secret*, is praised by critics around the world, and he continues to regularly deliver suspenseful novels you can't put down.

Sign up to his mailing list today and be the first to hear about upcoming releases and hot new deals for existing books. You'll also receive a FREE digital copy of *The Couple Downstairs* – an unputdownable domestic thriller you won't find anywhere else in the world.

www.ajcarterbooks.com/subscribe

Printed in Great Britain
by Amazon